Eleanor
& Abel

Also by Annette Sanford

Crossing Shattuck Bridge
Lasting Attachments

Eleanor & Abel

A ROMANCE

Annette Sanford

arrow books

Published by Arrow in 2003

3 5 7 9 0 8 6 4 2

First published in the United States by Counterpoint,
a member of the Perseus Books Group in 2003.

Arrow Books
The Random House Group Limited
20 Vauxhall Bridge Road, London, SW1V 2SA

Random House Australia (Pty) Limited
20 Alfred Street, Milsons Point, Sydney,
New South Wales 2061, Australia

Random House New Zealand Limited
18 Poland Road, Glenfield
Auckland 10, New Zealand

Random House (Pty) Limited
Endulini, 5a Jubilee Road, Parktown 2193, South Africa

The Random House Group Limited Reg. No. 954009

www.randomhouse.co.uk

A CIP catalogue record for this book
is available from the British Library

Papers used by Random House are natural, recyclable products made
from wood grown in sustainable forests. The manufacturing processes
conform to the environmental regulations of the country of origin

Printed and bound in Great Britain by
Bookmarque Ltd, Croydon, Surrey

ISBN 0 09 946557 4

*For Shannon Ravenel, with love
and appreciation for years of encouragement.
Special thanks to Rick and Mary Gardiner,
and David and Angela Adrian.*

1

Miss Eleanor Bannister owned a house on Florida Street she wanted to stop renting. She wanted to sell it. Or burn it down and collect the insurance, or let it go for taxes. She did not want to scrub the walls again and rake the muck out of the kitchen and lay down new linoleum and fix the faucets.

So when the man called up she said, "You could probably get a room over in Payne. Seven miles away. A larger town."

The man wasn't interested. "Sounds to me like sleeping on nails."

"Like what? A nice place like Payne?" Then she got his meaning. He was thinking *Pain!* A homonym! Forty years of teaching language in the Grover Public Schools, and she'd never noticed. Chagrined, she said, "It's spelled with a *y*."

"Oh, I see." He seemed pleased about it. "I had a relative once, Payne with a *y*."

He cleared a gravelly throat. "The thing is, I don't want a room. I want a house with a yard. I like to mow grass."

He was crazy. Or young. "There's a yard," she said patiently, "but it isn't all grass." Most of it was weeds. The back part was bushes that formed a little thicket where redbirds nested. Owls took shelter there. On cloudy days it got black as night inside that thicket. "It's hard work, you know, to keep a yard looking nice."

Hers didn't, not the Florida Street yard or her own that backed up to the thicket and ran on down to Tennessee. The yards hadn't looked nice since Mr. Cooper had gotten lame and she had to hire a boy who didn't know beans.

"I don't mind hard work," the man replied. "And I have plenty of time."

You are *young*, she thought, *and probably a drifter*. She closed the conversation. "I don't want to rent, but thank you for calling."

He answered politely, "Thank you, ma'am," and hung up the phone.

After supper Eleanor told Grace about the call when she came across the street to help pick figs. "It was unfriendly of me. New people moving in. I know they need houses."

"But you need to sell."

"I don't *need* to, Grace." Grace was trying again to find out about her finances, if she had any money beyond her teacher retirement. "I'm just tired of taking care of it, getting broken things fixed and dealing with deadbeats."

"He might not be a deadbeat. You could hardly tell over the telephone."

"He sounded very nice."

"He looked nice too."

"What do you mean?"

"I saw him at Maggie's." Grace's niece across town. "I drove over there to see if she had any eggs and to find out about Sissy—Maggie's girl, you know—to see if she'd had her baby. When I got out of my car he was getting into his truck. Abel Brown," Grace said. "String-bean type. Cap on his head."

"Well, if this isn't funny! What did Maggie say?"

"Said no more eggs till the weather cools off."

"I mean about Mr. Brown."

"Don't you care about the baby?"

"Grace—yes. Here, give me that bucket. We'll go up on the porch and have a talk."

"This is my bucket, Eleanor. I brought it from home. And what about these figs? If you leave them till morning, you won't have a one a bird hasn't pecked."

"All right, then. We'll talk while we pick."

They didn't, though. What settled the matter was a wasp that stung Grace on the end of her elbow and sent her home.

She called back in a little while to say she hadn't died of anaphylactic shock.

Eleanor was in bed with the radio on. "I'm glad to hear it."

"You can laugh if you want to, but it happens all the time. People's throats swell up and they can't catch their breath."

"If you were worried, Grace, you should have said so."

"I wasn't worried. I've been stung by wasps ten thousand times. What I'm calling to tell you is to lock up your house. Maggie told that Brown man where you live. Straight through the block from the Florida house. On Tennessee. A woman alone."

"Did she tell him that too?"

"I don't know if she did, but it's in the phone book. Eleanor Bannister. Does that sound alone?"

It did, thought Eleanor. Alone and lonely. Once you started to think about it, you might not stop. "I don't think I have to worry. You said he looked nice."

"You can't tell a thing by how somebody looks. And something else, Eleanor. My great-niece Sissy, Maggie's girl, you know, had a baby girl last Wednesday morning at four o'clock and nobody called."

"Would you have wanted them to at four o'clock?"

"They could have waited till seven. Instead they waited two days and I still had to go and find out myself. After all the presents I've given that girl."

"I'm sorry, Grace. I expect they forgot in their excitement."

"Well, don't you forget about locking up."

"I lock my doors every night at nine."

"I lock mine at eight. Earlier than that if there's a strange man in town, nosing around."

"You never did tell me why Mr. Brown was at Maggie's."

"He wasn't *at* Maggie's, Eleanor. He was out on the sidewalk. That's all there was to it."

"Did he stop just to chat?"

"He stopped," said Grace, "to ask about the rent house next door to Maggie."

"The Blackman house? He wouldn't want that."

"That's what Maggie told him. Then she told him about your place."

"You can tell her next time that my place is for sale."

"Tell her yourself. She'd love to hear from her favorite teacher."

"Her favorite teacher was Isabel Martin."

"Well, I can't argue about it now. My program is on."

"Do you think I'm keeping you? You called me!"

After Grace hung up, Eleanor turned off the radio and took a book from her night table. *The London Stalker,* checked out of the county library in Payne at the urging of the librarian: "It's not the kind of book you ordinarily read, Miss Bannister, but the suspense—oh my! You won't be able to put it down until the last page."

Miss Grimley rarely expressed an opinion about anything, so Eleanor, rather than mention her preference for choosing her own reading material, slipped *The London Stalker* into her book bag with the rest of her week's checkouts and went on her way. She had no intention of even dipping into *The Stalker,* but before the week was out she had exhausted her other selections, and now here she was on Thursday, one night to go and nothing to read.

Opening the book, she scanned the first page. Pure claptrap. On page two a young woman named Enid was stabbed in the heart. Page three gave the bloody details.

Certainly not a bedtime story. Nor any other kind worth wasting her energy on. Eleanor tossed the book back onto the table and snapped off her light.

Immediately a dog began barking. The Yanceys' boxer that never made a sound during the day so it could spend all night keeping the neighborhood awake.

Maybe tonight it was directing its bark at the Grover Stalker, Eleanor mused. Grace's string-bean man roaming around, inspecting exteriors of houses on Tennessee. He would find it a disappointing venture if he had robbery in mind. He would do better across the highway in a more affluent area than the blocks of modest houses that had sprung up around Eleanor's comfortable old family home four or five years ago when Corn Products had opened on the coast and spilled the overflow of its employees into sleepy little Grover, fourteen miles inland.

Mr. Brown would hardly be interested in Main Street either. One stoplight, the bank on the corner, the cleaners next to it. Then Dottie's Flowers and the dentist's office with an alley between. The men's clothing store her father had once owned. The bakery. The drugstore. Eleanor yawned, thinking of the dozen or so smaller businesses before the railroad track, and about the same number from there to the highway.

Grover, Texas, where without intending to she had spent her whole life, except her college years; where she was recognized everywhere as Miss Eleanor Bannister, teacher, spinster. Maiden lady, her mother would have preferred.

Eleanor yawned again, making no effort to conceal her presence from Mr. String Bean Brown if he happened to be squatting beneath her window. A sigh followed the yawn. A single woman was what she was. What she had chosen to be. And chosen correctly.

Then she was asleep, little ripples of breath passing between her lips while the dog barked on and half a moon swung across the sky.

2

Eleanor got up at daybreak to finish picking the figs. She went out in her nightgown to the side of the garage and stood in the wet grass without any shoes. She intended to pick the front of the tree first and be around back by the time the paper boy passed, but before that could happen a pickup truck turned into the driveway.

A man got out. Tall and slender. Cap on his head. "Good morning, ma'am."

Eleanor stared, something she had taught children never to do.

"Excuse the hour." He crossed the grass. "But I saw you were out."

Out in her nightgown! But at least it wasn't a flimsy see-through. "I came out early to beat the birds."

He nodded approvingly. "Birds do love figs." He was a man about seventy. Or seventy-five. On the telephone he had sounded forty.

How had she sounded?

She stood up straight, like a woman, she hoped, who was wearing underwear. "Mr. Brown," she said. She was pleased to see him jump. "As I mentioned on the phone, I'm not renting my house. I plan to sell it."

"With a hole in the roof?"

Eleanor jumped.

He said more gently, "You didn't hear the wind? Blowing hard in the night?"

She hadn't heard anything, hadn't woken up until the clock in the living room was striking six.

"A good-sized limb struck your porch."

"A limb," she said. Why couldn't it have been lightning? "I'd better go see." She set off grimly in the direction of the thicket.

Brown came after her. "We'll go in my truck." Without laying a finger on her, he herded her toward it and got her in.

She came to her senses when he slammed the door. "Wait!" she said. "I have to go in the house and get my wrapper."

"And hunt for your slippers. And stop by the mirror and comb your hair." He backed the truck. "Just sit tight. This won't take a minute."

"On the phone," she said, "you had a few manners."

"You can take a quick look and I'll bring you right back."

She sat speechless beside him until they rounded the corner and she saw her house, a child's drawing of a house: the front-door mouth, two windows for eyes. "I don't see a limb."

"You can see it better from the back." He drove around. "Look up yonder." The limb lay on the roof like a torn-off leg.

"I don't see a hole."

"It's one the size of a skateboard. I climbed up and looked."

"You climbed my roof?"

"On a ladder, of course. I carry a ladder." He pointed a thumb toward the bed of the truck, to saws and hammers and everything else.

"Are you a carpenter?"

"I can do carpenter work. And painting and such. I can fix this rip for next to nothing. There's plenty of shingles in your garage."

"You went in my garage?"

"And also in the storeroom. Looking for decking." He shot her a grin. "Found some too."

"Mr. Brown," she said, "you haven't been hired." She was nearly naked and foolishly seated in this man's truck, but she said it anyway, and said something else. "What are you up to?"

He looked straight at her. "Up to filling my time."

She had stared down enough schoolboys to think she could believe him. "You've been riding around this morning searching for damages?"

"On the chance. Yes, ma'am."

"Stop calling me ma'am! I'm not a hundred."

"Didn't think you were." His blue eyes twinkled. "Thought you might be seventy."

"That's wrong too." But it was close enough to give her a shiver. "If I hired you for this job, when can you start?"

"In the next five minutes."

"How much will you charge?"

"A fair and honest price. I can promise you that."

"Make it fifty dollars and you can do it."

"Make it sixty-five, depending on the decking. And extra, of course, if I have to buy nails."

Eleanor walked home. She insisted on that in case Grace, as usual, was looking out a window. She told Abel Brown she walked around barefoot to strengthen her arches, but on the path through the thicket the lie about killed her. She had to sit down twice, once on the bench where she read her devotionals and one more time on the stump of an ash tree, where fire ants bit her on both sets of toes and up one ankle.

When she got back to her house, she took a cold bath mixed with baking soda and didn't eat breakfast until a quarter of nine.

"I'm all off schedule," she told Grace when she called up to see why Eleanor was at home and not at the library.

"It's Friday, you know."

"I'm leaving right now." She drove around the block. Mr. Brown wasn't visible, but his truck was there. She said out loud, "Sixty-five dollars. Mr. Abel Brown must think money is water."

In Payne she discovered the library closed. For roof repairs. "Wind damage," said a man standing on the sidewalk.

She drove home bitterly and went to the store for fire-ant bait and lemons and sugar and jars for preserves. She had to go back for corn pads and Tums and to stop at the post office and run by the bank. At one o'clock she started on the figs.

The first batch scorched because Grace telephoned to see who was hammering.

"Mr. Brown is at your rent house? What's he doing there?"

Eleanor explained, leaving out the nightgown. "I have to go, Grace. I'm cooking preserves."

"Did you peel the figs?"

"I like the peeling left on."

"Tell me this, do you think he's handsome?"

Eleanor heard the lawn mower some time later. She had paraffin melting on the stove and couldn't go out. At four-thirty she was crossing her lawn (beautifully cut) and passing through the thicket, where she threw down ant bait. Emerging at the rent house, she found the grass mowed there, the roof mended, and the truck leaving with the broken-off limb.

"Mr. Brown!" she called.

Mr. Brown hopped out. "Miss Bannister," he said, "you're wearing shoes."

"A few hours barefoot is all it takes." She saw that Grace was right; he was a nice-looking man, in an elderly way. And a gentleman too, or else he would have mentioned clothes as well as shoes.

"The roof looks nice," Eleanor told him.

"It's going to look better when those new shingles weather."

"You mowed both lawns."

"I like mowing lawns."

"You're hauling off the limb."

"That's part of the roof job."

"Well, that's very accommodating," Eleanor said.

"Well. I'll see you tomorrow."

Her brain spun around. "Tomorrow? What for? I'll pay you now." She opened her purse, a little snap-mouthed affair her mother had once carried. A miser's purse, Grace liked to call it. "How much do I owe you?"

"No hurry," he said. "One or two things still need to be done."

"You've done too much. More than I'm paying for."

"Step around here. I'll show you something."

He pointed out the screens. "These screens are torn."

"I've noticed," she said.

"Have you noticed the steps?" He put a foot through one without the least effort. "It's things like this that bring down the price when you sell a place."

"I know, Mr. Brown, but I'm not putting money into this house."

"You have to put money in to get money out."

Eleanor sighed. This sweet little house had been her parents' honeymoon cottage. Hers, too, she had once imagined. Had she imagined it since? Maybe one or two times before she was fifty. Or whenever it was her periods stopped.

"Look," Mr. Brown said. Another step crumbled.

If she burned the place down, she might go to jail. "How much would it cost, the screens and steps?"

Abel Brown clutched his throat. "I'll be glad to tell you over a drink of water."

Mr. Brown stayed for supper.

He played the violin. Her father's violin she kept on a shelf in the living room. She sat him down in there because the kitchen was a wreck, jars of fig preserves all over the drainboard, dirty pots in the sink, and shiny places on the floor their shoes stuck to.

He didn't play well. Old strings, he said, but he brought out a certain note now and then that put a lump in her throat, and she let him go on though it drove her crazy.

She apologized ten times for having him work all day without any water. He told her eleven times he did have water. He had a whole jug full, but he drank it all up. He'd only been dry, he said, for thirty minutes.

Thirty minutes was too long, Eleanor said. He had the largest feet she had ever seen. Size sixteen was what she guessed. Big hands too, floating over the violin, tucking it under his chin.

He stopped playing at last and told her quietly, "I'm going to get your supper."

"Why, what do you mean?" She jumped out of the chair where she had been sort of dozing, going up a ladder into somebody's attic.

"You can't cook in that kitchen."

She didn't tell him she hadn't intended to. She ate cereal for supper with a banana sliced over it. Tonight she had planned to eat a cantaloupe.

"Where will you get it?" she croaked out.

"I'll drive over to Payne."

"Seven miles," she marveled.

"There's a deli over there at a convenience store."

He had learned a lot about Payne since yesterday. "It's not a big deli."

He laughed out loud. "Do you want a big supper?"

In her embarrassment she said, "Get enough for yourself."

While he was gone, she slammed things around and cleaned up the kitchen. She put a cloth on the table and got out napkins. Feeling like a fool, she went outside and picked a bouquet of blue plumbago, knowing while she did it that the blossoms would drop off and prickly stuff underneath would latch on to everything.

Of course Grace was out, picking up twigs the storm had thrown down. She called across the street, "Did you finish your figs?"

"Yes, they're fine."

"I'll come have a look."

"I'm expecting Mr. Brown in just a few minutes."

"Mr. Brown?" Grace halted.

"I have to pay him for his work."

"Are you giving him flowers?"

"I'm trimming the bush."

"Oh," said Grace. "Well, have a good time."

Eleanor did enjoy herself. Up to a point.

Mr. Brown brought shrimp, boiled and peeled, and potato salad. Men, she had been told, love potato salad. She seldom bought it, and never in hot weather for fear of ptomaine. Possibly the shrimp were tainted too, though they tasted all right. If later in the night she had to get up and go to the hospital, she had a clean gown and an insurance policy.

"Miss Eleanor," Brown said when he had eaten the cantaloupe she served for dessert, "driving over to Payne I had a thought about your house."

"Did you?" she said. They had drunk a little wine from an old green bottle she had opened at Christmas, and now he was filling their glasses again.

"You know I live in a trailer."

She didn't know, but she said, "How nice."

"It's not any bigger than a sardine can. I haven't been out of it for more than a year."

"You've been traveling?" she said.

"Traveling all over."

"What made you stop here?"

"I came down the highway and saw the lake."

Full of dirty brown water, Eleanor thought. If she were able to travel, she would go to the mountains.

"I'm parked at that camp next to the bridge. It's not a bad spot, but I'm sick of that trailer."

Eleanor sipped wine. "I can't rent you my house. I'm sorry, Abel." *Abel*, she heard! Heard it leap from her lips like a frog in a fairy tale.

"Eleanor." He smiled. "I'm going to help you sell it."

"Are you in real estate too?"

"I have a proposition."

"A *proposition!*" In her mother's day, ladies slapped men for that.

"A business deal." He patted her hand, which she picked up quickly and put under the table. "I worked it out on the way to Payne."

She calmed down slowly when she heard what it was.

He had an idea he would live in her house. Instead of paying rent he would renovate it.

"Insane," she said.

"Room by room. I'll start in the kitchen. I'll tear out the sink and then the cabinets."

"You'll do no such thing."

"You can't sell a house that's falling down and get anything for it."

"I'll sell it that way or not at all."

"Just listen a minute."

"No," she said.

He got the violin and picked out a few notes. "It's a honeymoon cottage."

She came to attention. "How did you know?"

"They all have that look."

"There are others?" she said.

"Maybe none quite as nice." He put down the violin and tried her preserves from a dish on the stove left out as a sample. "Is there lemon in this?"

"Of course there's lemon."

"But no vanilla."

"Certainly not."

He sat down again and said like a grandfather, "Eleanor, you have a fine house you're letting rot down."

Her throat tightened again. "How can I help it?"

"You didn't listen. I'm offering free my priceless labor."

"And materials?" she said. "Are those free too? If I wanted to do it, I can't spare the money."

"Borrow it, dear."

"I never borrow."

"Your credit's no good?"

"I don't owe a cent and never intend to."

"Oh, too bad." He seemed truly sorry. "You're squeezing your pennies and letting your dollars run out the door."

"I have supported myself for a good many years."

"And nicely, I'm sure, but you might have done better if you'd sold this big house and moved to the small one."

"You're full of ideas."

"Good ones too." He plucked again on the strings of the violin. "Do you know that song? 'The Beautiful Old Things'?"

"No, I don't."

"I don't either. I wish I did." He got out of his chair and strolled to the door. "Thank you, Miss El, for an interesting evening. You'll understand if I move along now."

"Wait," she said. "I want to give you your money." She turned around to get it. When she turned back he was already gone.

3

Eleanor didn't sleep all night after her encounter with Abel Brown. Her thoughts ran amok like squirrels in an attic. She got up at four and went out to the kitchen to clear a place in the pantry to put the preserves. Then she mopped the floor and sat in the dark with the violin. At the first sign of day she put on her wrapper and slippers and went to the thicket.

Above her bench a redbird was singing.

"*Cheer up,* yourself!" she told the bird. "You don't have a house that's falling down. Or a head like a pumpkin from Christmas wine." She stared at her feet, speckled with ant bites. What should she do? Keep saving her money for Death with Dignity? Keep putting aside for the Lingering Illness, for women coming in to cook and clean and trim her chin whiskers and privately bathe her?

Or should she blow it? Spend it all reviving the cottage? New sinks, new screens, no telling what.

Was it only yesterday she was picking figs when Abel Brown drove up in her yard?

He drove up now. In the rent-house yard. She saw through the bushes his descent from the truck, his strides toward the porch. He began prying boards off the steps. Like he owned the place!

She jumped up and burst through the yaupon. "What are you doing?"

"This has to be fixed." He seemed unsurprised that she had appeared. "I'm doing it now and getting it done with."

She saw a diagrammed sentence up in the air, *with* dangling off like an extra foot. "It's the Sabbath," she said.

"Can't a fellow pull nails out of boards on the Sabbath?"

"People are sleeping!"

"I bet in Payne they're not." He laughed at his pun. "All right. Come on. Let's go and drink coffee till the sleepers get up."

"This is twice you've pulled this," Eleanor complained. He was toasting bread without even asking.

"You don't really mind, do you, Miss El?" He buttered the toast and spread on figs. "What's going to happen to all those jars of this wonderful stuff?"

"I give them for Christmas."

"That's a long way off. Christmas," he said.

"You may take one now if that's what you're wanting."

"That's it, all right. Cold winter mornings, figs'll sure taste good."

Eleanor sat and wondered: Where will he be when winter comes on? In Florida maybe. *Or in the Florida Street house?* She saw it happening like a train bearing down on Eleanor Bannister tied to the tracks.

"I told you a lie," she said without meaning to.

"About your money?" He looked over his cup. "You have some, do you?"

"Of course I do. A woman alone. Who would look after me?"

"The government," he said and poured more coffee. "Or some good man."

"I'm past all that."

"You are if you think so." He sat back and grinned. "If you found the right man you could be Porch-Bannister."

She answered him, bristling. "Funnier still, I could be Brown-Bannister."

"Miss El!" he said. "Do you want to discuss it?"

"Certainly not!"

"That's worse than *ma'am,* saying *certainly not* all the time." He went to the pantry. "Did you say two jars?"

He came out with three. "I lied to you too." He set the jars on the tabletop. "I didn't plan the renovation on the way to buy supper. I planned it all day, even down to the colors. Confederate blue in both the bedrooms. White on the woodwork." He went a step further. "Crazy quilts on the beds."

She turned from the sink, where she was washing the dishes. "This is going too far."

"Yup, it is. It's way out of hand." He crossed to her side. "Are the church people up? Or should I go on to Payne and come back later?"

She dried her hands. "I'll pay you what I owe you, and there won't be any need to come back at all."

A stillness came over him. "If that's how you want it, it's sixty dollars."

"Did you have to buy decking?"

"Nails have gone up."

She took her snap-mouthed purse out of a cabinet. "I'm paying you seventy-five. You mowed both lawns."

"Suit yourself, but I might say this. I wouldn't keep cash like that in the house."

"I'm not afraid."

"You never can tell who might walk in the door."

A string-bean man. A cap on his head. "Thank you, Mr. Brown, for fixing the roof."

"My pleasure, ma'am." He saluted her sadly. "Ever need a good kiss, give me a call."

4

Eleanor went around all day calling Mr. Brown names. Impertinent jackass. Impudent fool. She avoided Grace by not going to church. In the late afternoon she slipped off to Payne and went to the movies. And then ate shrimp and potato salad.

He would come back, of course. To get his preserves.

By Tuesday he hadn't. Wednesday either.

She got in her car and drove to the bridge. Across the water she could see the trailers lined up in the camp. Which was his? Where was his truck?

She came home and telephoned.

The attendant told her he had pulled out on Monday.

"What's the matter with you?" Grace asked at the start of the next week, standing in Eleanor's kitchen, her eyes wide open like a questioning cow's.

"Nothing is the matter."

"You haven't been at church two Sundays in a row. You haven't swept the sidewalk, and now you're mending. You never pick up a needle unless you're sick."

"Sewing makes me sick."

"So why are you doing it?"

They went into the living room and sat on the couch, Eleanor discommoded by the violin not being in its place and Grace agog at this turn of events.

"Mr. Brown," said Eleanor, "has moved on."

"Mr. Brown? Well, I hope so! Did you run him off?"

"I set him straight and he took offense."

"Good for you! A brazen man like that, making himself at home the first minute he met you. I saw right away he couldn't be trusted."

"You don't even know him."

"I've seen him, Eleanor."

"On the sidewalk at Maggie's."

"In and out of your house."

"You spied on us, Grace?"

"Of course. Wouldn't you?"

Eleanor brought cake and warmed-over coffee. She made a clean breast of things. Half clean anyway, omitting the nightgown and the kissing remark.

"So the problem," said Grace, "is he tore up your steps and left without fixing them?"

"That's part of it, yes." Eleanor pinned her gaze on a sepia photo of her great-aunt Helen. "The other part is, I've started to miss him."

"Miss him!" said Grace.

"His coming and going. He livened things up."

"Well, of course he did. And don't think he didn't know it! A woman alone like you is a sitting duck for a man like him."

"You're alone."

"I have family, Eleanor, to keep track of me. You haven't anyone."

"True," said Eleanor. Aunt Helen, she saw, had begun to fade badly. Much like herself, she thought with a tremor. "It is also true that I have suffered a loss—Mr. Brown going off without even telling me."

Grace's eyes opened wider. "Oh, my dear—"

"It's nothing to pity." Eleanor sat up straighter. "What I have had is a lapse. Natural, I think, for a woman my age who has never been married, who has never cared to be involved in any way with a man." She plucked a thread from her skirt. "But now, late in life—"

"You're seventy, aren't you? Or seventy-one?"

"Now, late in life, a kind of panic sets in."

"A panic?" said Grace.

"Panic and worse. A dormant silliness."

"A what?"

"A silliness that has waked up all at once and wants to dance."

"Dance!" exclaimed Grace.

"Wants to kick up its heels! Haven't you ever felt that?"

"No! Well—" Grace reddened. "Well, maybe I did once. After Roger died. There was a butcher at Four Star who had lovely lips."

"Lips?" said Eleanor, thrown off the track.

"I used to dream of those lips, coming down on mine." Grace folded her hands across her stomach. "His name was Fritz."

"I remember a Fred."

"That might have been it."

"What happened, Grace?"

"It passed without consequence."

Eleanor said quietly, "This might pass."

"It will. Give it time. You can't know a man in only two days."

"Ten," said Eleanor.

"Ten?" Grace frowned.

"Here, Grace. Have more cake."

"I believe I will. It's delicious, Eleanor. Did you bake it for him?"

"It's been in the freezer since the last bake sale."

"In that case," said Grace, "I think I baked it. Yes, I did. I always put curlicues on my icing." She picked up her fork. "I know what would help, Eleanor. If you were to see Mr. Brown as I saw him."

"Oh, I don't think so."

Grace insisted. Her view of the matter was that Abel Brown was a competent con man whose chief aim was to get the cottage.

"Get it?" said Eleanor. "What do you mean?"

"Own it," said Grace. "Fix it up and sell it and scoot out of town."

Eleanor felt better, hearing this nonsense. "He couldn't sell it. I have the deed."

"He could marry you, couldn't he?"

"If I were drugged and shackled!"

"You're sounding more and more like a woman in love."

"It isn't love! It's not even affection. If it's anything, it's loneliness, Grace."

"I'm lonely too. But I wouldn't dive off the high board just to cure it."

"No cures were offered."

"You're lucky there. Look how he worked things. Smooth as a tick's back, mowing your lawn, staying for supper."

"Schemes, do you think? Right at the start I asked what he was up to."

"What did he say?"

"He likes to fill his time."

Grace snickered. "Any fool can lie. He looked like a man who would stop at nothing."

"How could you tell?"

"By the way he walked."

"Oh yes, I see. One foot, then the other."

"Surely you noticed. Every step he took showed how cocky he was."

"He is not cocky! He simply knows his job. His confidence is justified."

"Has he told you how he's spent his life? What he's done up to now to fill his time?"

"He's been traveling," said Eleanor.

"I'll bet he has! When he's kicked out of one place he goes to another."

"I have no information to indicate that."

"Use your common sense, Eleanor!"

"I'm surprised you think I have any."

"You have more than I do. Of the two of us, Eleanor, you're the practical one. I rely on you."

"After today, you'll think twice about that."

"I won't," said Grace. "This has been a good talk. It's made you seem more human."

"I didn't before?"

"Not as much as most people. You always have answers to everything."

"Grace, that's ridiculous."

"It's not your fault. Teaching does it. Teachers get bossy."

"It's getting late, Grace. It's time for supper."

"Are you asking me to eat or telling me to leave?" Grace put her plate aside. "Whichever, I'm going. It's Bingo night."

She turned around at the door. "We're much closer now, aren't we? May I call you Ellie?"

"Not today," said Eleanor. "Probably never."

"There," said Grace. "That's what I mean."

For the next few days Eleanor went around in her wrapper, reading old letters and playing the piano. She put a Vicks plaster on her chest and then peeled it off.

On Friday she dressed and went to the library.

Abel Brown was there. She didn't know it. She wandered around, reading blurbs on the novels, until somebody said, "Here's Mr. Brown's water. Who's going to take it?"

"Mr. Brown who?" It popped out like a frog.

"Up on the roof."

"I'll take it," she said. "I'm going that way."

He had barely come down before she was after him.

"It's too high up there for a man of your age!"

"Why, Miss El," he said, "you've put on your shoes and stepped out of your bailiwick."

"Because I read," she told him severely.

"I read too. That's how I found out there was work over here."

"Are you living in Payne? "

"Payne with a *y*?" Abel grinned. "I'm at the Family Campground. I'm slightly out of place, but nevertheless." He shook sweat from his brow. "Is this water for me?"

She steered him to a tree. "Are you trying to kill yourself? It's ninety degrees."

"It's a hundred and twenty up on the roof."

"Then quit and go home!"

"I'd rather die up there than be cooped up somewhere in a nursing facility."

"You aren't ready to die."

"The trouble is, when you do get ready, they rarely let you."

Eleanor pressed on. "You forgot your preserves."

He lifted gray eyebrows. "Is it safe to come get them?"

"Come about four. You can fix the steps."

5

Driving home from the library, Eleanor thought, *What in heaven's name am I doing, involving myself again with Abel Brown? I haven't slept well since I met him. I haven't eaten well. I've confided in Grace, and by now Maggie and Sissy, and maybe the whole town, know my personal affairs.*

What personal affairs? her brain responded. *The books you've read? What you eat for breakfast?*

"This is not a scoffing matter!" Eleanor's distressed gaze fell on the flat fields beyond the window: heads of maize not quite russet, young rice plants nodding beside the road.

Abel Brown, she lamented, *has robbed me of my peace. I could have gone on forever, a desiccated seed rattling happily in a shriveling pod. But he had to climb up on my roof and pour water on me—and now I'm sprouting, way past my season!*

Tears threatening, she steered the car off the road onto an unpaved shoulder. "I will not weep on a public highway!"

She fixed a sightless stare on earthen irrigation dikes snaking through the nearest field, on the cloudless sky stretching toward the horizon. Toward Payne.

I only asked him to come and fix the cottage steps.

You asked him to supper. And it won't stop there.

A tractor sputtered up behind the car. In the rearview mirror she saw a man jumping down, approaching her window, tapping on the glass.

"Something wrong, Miz Bannister?"

Eleanor stared at his suntanned face, trying to place him. She rolled down the window and let in a blast of hot air. "Not a thing wrong," she answered as cheerily as she could. "I just stopped for a minute to admire this beautiful field."

David. *David Witcher!* He had always seated himself far from her desk, looking out the window, cleaning his fingernails. She hadn't given David Witcher a thought since his last report card. Thirty-five years ago. Maybe forty. "Is this your land, David?"

"No'm, it's rented. But that's my crop." He beamed with pleasure. "You'll have to come around in August when it's really looking good, the heads filled out and all." His broad face clouded. "If it makes," he said. "Sometimes it don't."

"Why not?" she asked.

"Things get after it. It's fine in the morning, and by evening it's ruint."

"What kinds of things?" Shamed by her ignorance.

"Bugs!" he exclaimed. "Stinkbugs, army worms, cinchbugs. Diseases!" he said. He named them on thick, soiled fingers. "Sheath blight, stem rot. Smut!"

"But aren't there preventives? Insecticides and such?"

"Oh yes, ma'am. But if the humidity ain't right, they don't do no good. There's things go wrong you'd never think of. And then come the blackbirds, and you can't do nothing if a hurricane blows in before cutting time."

Humbled, Eleanor gazed at the rippling field, picturing in its place the bare, plowed soil of months before. "I'm sure it's very hard work out here in the sun."

David grinned at Eleanor. "If I'd listened to you, studied harder, I could be sitting in an air-conditioned office, playing the boss."

"Would you prefer that, David?"

"God, no! I mean, no ma'am. That's one thing I can't stand, being cooped up."

Eleanor understood the feeling. Years of watching cars passing her schoolroom window. Women chatting on the sidewalk down by the church, holding grocery bags. Until her retirement she had never been free to shop on weekday mornings, never gotten in her car and driven off somewhere, just for the fun of it. She knew quite a lot about being cooped up, and not only at school.

She started the engine. "Thank you, David, for informing me about your work. It was a great pleasure looking at your field."

"I've got six more!" he said heartily. "You come back and I'll put you on my tractor and we'll have a look at all of 'em!"

Eleanor rolled up the window and waved good-bye. Thirty-five years ago she wouldn't have given five cents for David Witcher's chances of succeeding at anything.

The rest of the morning she busied herself around the house, spirits lifted from seeing her former pupil and what he had accomplished. He had come from a family with little money. The Witchers, people said, on the dole again. Where had he gotten the nerve to set out as a farmer? Someone had offered him an opportunity, and he had had the courage to take it. "He took the ball and ran with it," she said aloud happily.

She herself rarely took chances. A sobering thought that dispersed her mood of gaiety.

She went into the living room and sat on the couch. She loved this house, loved this room. The old piano. Shelves crowded with her father's books. But she was conscious all at once of a mustiness surrounding her, the stifling smells of age, of windows kept shut too long and drapes drawn to preserve the colors in a rug that had grown dim anyway.

I'll die here, she thought. No one in Grover would expect anything else.

She was half asleep, dozing on the couch, when she heard truck noise and went into the kitchen to see if Abel was at the cottage.

She saw him through the trees, unloading lumber from the back of his pickup. She watched him squat by the steps, measuring, whistling, she imagined, scratching his head. Soon the sound of an electric saw rang out.

Eleanor fixed a picnic and took it out when the hammering stopped. She meant for them to eat on the cottage lawn, but they ate in the thicket because an early thrush mixed up on the seasons was singing its heart out and she wanted to hear.

They sat on her bench and spread the food on a folding table.

"This is good," Abel said about the baked beans and wieners.

"Try some of this." Mustard chow-chow she had made herself.

With the meal under way, she made an announcement. "I have halfway decided you can live in my house."

"Halfway?" he said.

"I have to know first if you're a con man."

He whooped at that. "Do you think if I was I'd tell you yes?"

"Are you or aren't you? Tell me straight."

"I am not a con man."

"You understand, don't you, what I mean by that?"

"I think I do. A liar and a cheat who might slicker you out of whatever you own."

"That's it exactly." She folded her hands. "And you say you aren't? Can I believe you?"

"It's the truth, Eleanor. Would you pass the grapes?"

She ate the banana she had previously intended to slice over cereal and eat in the kitchen. "Grace says it all fits together for you to be crooked."

"Grace." He frowned. "Grace from across the street? Who ducks into the garage when she thinks I've seen her?"

"She thinks your walk gives you away, that you were smooth as a tick's back, the way you worked me."

He nodded agreeably. "I did some of that."

"Mowing the lawns? Bringing me supper?"

"And playing the violin. I thought you'd enjoy it."

"You didn't play well."

"I played well enough to put you to sleep." He ate a cracker. "I worked you another time, to get the preserves."

"Grace thinks you want to get my house."

"I want to live in it a while and see how it feels to get out of that trailer."

"What if you like it?"

"Maybe I'll buy it."

"Do you have any money?"

"Enough," he said.

The bird sang again from a farther place, whistling purer than air or water.

Eleanor said, "What have you been doing for most of your life?"

"Smoking, for one thing. But I gave it up." He leaned back and thought. "I drank some too." He grinned at Eleanor. "Till I got thrown in jail."

"Jail!" she exclaimed.

"Creating a disturbance in a public place. I poured a pitcher of beer over a smart aleck's head. He hit me in the jaw. And of course I hit him back." He smiled, pleased. "And one other time, when I was really stupid, I sold some bogus insurance and got locked up again."

Eleanor pushed her plate away. "You have an unsavory past."

"A few unsavory pages in a long history. Nothing unusual. Most people get into scrapes now and then."

"Not scrapes that violate the law! Not the people I know."

"Maybe the people you know didn't get caught."

"What a cynical remark!"

Abel nodded. "It was, wasn't it? I guess getting cynical is something else I've done, along with drilling oil wells and building houses. Mostly, though"—his grin came back—"I've gone around looking. For more lawns to mow. What about you?"

Shaken, she murmured, "I've been right here. Teaching. And picking figs."

"Why didn't you marry?"

"Why should I marry? I was in love with teaching. And I had my parents."

He regarded her thoughtfully. "I've shocked you, haven't I? With my wicked past."

"You have dismayed me, Abel."

They sat in silence, watching lightning bugs come out of the grass.

"Beautiful," said Abel after a time.

"Wondrous," agreed Eleanor.

"Not the fireflies. I'm talking about you." He turned to look at her. "It's beautiful the way you live your life. So certain of everything. So undisturbed."

"In a vacuum?" said Eleanor. "Is that what you mean?"

"I mean in a straightforward way that I've missed out on. I admire your ability to handle your difficulties."

Eleanor blinked. "I can have quite a temper."

"In the schoolroom, I imagine."

"No, never there. If I could possibly help it. Havoc creates havoc. Where children are involved, the adult in charge must behave like an adult."

Abel gazed unfocused through the thicket. "A good many adults never learn that lesson."

Eleanor plucked a leaf from a stripling mulberry and folded it neatly. "Have you given any thought to the shape of the year?"

"The year?" He chuckled. "I can't say I have."

"Have you never noticed that it's winter on one end and on the other end too?"

He took her hand, like a child's hand in the palm of his, and squeezed it lightly. "If you were in charge, how would you arrange it?"

"I'd start with summer and end with spring." She let his thumb trace the moons of her fingernails, though her mouth was dry and her heart knocking. "Grace says—"

He gave a mild groan.

"She says I ought to know you longer before I trust you."

"You can tell Grace people our age can't waste time on long engagements."

"Engagements!" she said.

"Just a manner of speaking, Eleanor."

"We are not engaged."

"We are not," he agreed.

She let her heart calm down before she spoke again. "Have you ever been married?"

"Once," he said. "For about thirty minutes."

"Why didn't it last?"

"We didn't like each other."

She took a long breath: the dive off the high board Grace had mentioned. "Abel," she said, "you may live in my cottage if you tell me truthfully you have no interest in making a match."

"A match." He smiled. "You mean like a couple? Miss El," he said, "I will never legally or criminally seize your house."

"It's not the house alone." She went ahead fearfully. "It's what you might think because I'm letting you live in it."

"I might think you care for me."

"Yes," she said. "I wouldn't want to mislead you."

He chuckled again. "You *don't* care for me."

"I don't care for marriage."

"Would you care to explain?"

"I'm not sure I can."

"Try, why don't you?"

She started slowly and gathered steam. "I've lived by myself for too many years. I have to have my own room. I like to read late. I get up and take medicine. And I'm used to playing the radio all night if I want."

He waited quietly.

"And sex," she burst out with a bravery previously unknown to her. "The very idea of it gives me a stomach ache."

"Scares you," he said.

"Scares me to death."

They listened to the bird in the thicket again. When it flew, Abel said, "I've lived by myself most of my life. I need my own room. I watch TV until two in the morning. I get up and take walks. And sex at my age is not to be counted on."

"Well," said Eleanor, "I'm glad that's settled."

"It's good," he agreed, "to have it out of the way."

They sat a while longer. Then she began putting things in the picnic hamper.

"Would you like more tea?"

"Tea? No, thank you." He stopped her hands from folding the tablecloth. "Tell me again about your year."

"I'd start it in June."

"So that would mean that right about now it's the middle of January?"

"Yes." She smiled. "Can't you tell it's cooler?"

"By July, your time, I'll be through with the house. Is that long enough to get over a scare?"

"Six months? Oh, no. No, I don't think so."

"How long will it take?"

He felt her tremble. "Maybe till Christmas."

"Dear girl," he soothed, "July *is* Christmas."

"I mean next year."

"Miss El," he whispered. He put an arm around her. "I would never rush you, but by any calendar it's time we kissed."

"Abel! It's not dark yet!"

"Close your eyes, sweetheart, and you'll see that it is."

6

Grace called early the next morning. "Let's go over to Sissy's, say about ten, and see the baby. Then we'll stop and get bread at the Lutheran Ladies bake sale and go have lunch. Maybe at the Tea Room. Would you like lunch at the Tea Room?"

Eleanor, staring into the dresser mirror from the side of her bed, saw in the gray light how flat her chest was, how bony her shoulders. *Sweetheart,* he had said. Before he kissed her.

He *was* after something.

He was after her house, though he said he wasn't.

Said it convincingly.

"Eleanor, are you there?"

"Yes, Grace. I can't go today."

"If you're worried about a present, I crocheted extra booties. You can take a pair of those."

"I'm busy, Grace."

"You aren't busy. You aren't even up. Your paper is still out, lying on the sidewalk."

"It's only six o'clock!"

"I'll call back later."

"Don't call back! Mr. Brown is coming." She rushed past that. "I've given him permission to overhaul my rent house."

"Oh. I see."

"No, you don't see! It's exactly as I'm telling you. It's a business arrangement."

"I noticed last evening that he's back in town."

"He notices you too, Grace, when you duck into the garage and pretend you're not spying!"

"That's unkind, Eleanor."

"It is. I'm sorry. But that's why you're calling me at the crack of dawn, isn't it? To find out what we were doing in the thicket last night?"

"We're friends, aren't we, Eleanor? And you did confide in me how lonely you are."

"This is not the time, Grace, for this conversation."

"Where has Mr. Brown been?"

"Ask him, Grace! Hail him the next time you see him passing your house."

"A single woman, Eleanor, has to be careful. A woman like yourself, not acquainted with the vagaries of men."

"If you think *vagaries* means something vulgar, get your dictionary right now and look it up!"

Grace said hastily, "I'll put your paper on your porch. Unless Mr. Brown intends to do that."

"I will pick up my own paper! If you'll get off the phone."

Abel was tearing out the cottage sink when Eleanor entered the kitchen. "Oh, my heavens, you've already started!"

"Good morning, Miss El." He turned around, smiling. "I trust you had a good rest."

"Rest? Yes. Now, stop what you're doing. We need to talk about this." She had spent half an hour deciding what to wear. A flowered skirt or a plain one? Blue blouse or yellow?

"We talked about it last night."

"Tentatively. Nothing was settled."

He laid down his crowbar. "You've had second thoughts."

"And third ones and fourths."

He offered her a seat, a wooden crate with a lid. "I'll sit on the sawhorse."

She folded her hands in the lap of the flowered skirt. "I don't know what to say. I was a fool last night. A rash, silly fool."

"Carried away by the moonlight," he answered calmly.

"It was too early for a moon." Her face heated. "It was barely dusk."

"And you kissed me anyway."

"You kissed me!"

"I got the idea it was fairly mutual."

Eleanor tightened her lips. A classroom reflex. "It was premature."

"Ah," he said. "So what we need to do this morning is back up and start over."

"Yes." She breathed in. "Yes, we need to back up."

"Where? To the fig tree?"

"This is not a laughing matter."

"Oh, I'm not laughing. Let's see. You were out in your nightgown—"

"Stop it! Just stop it!"

"And you had no shoes on." He took her hand gently. "I fell in love right then."

Tears started in her eyes. "This whole thing is ridiculous. You're a silly fool too. Or else you're a con man like Grace says you are."

"I see what's happened." Quietly, softly. "This morning you woke up in your bed where you have slept all your life, and everything was different."

"Except Eleanor Bannister! I am sixty-nine years old," she said accusingly. "Sixty-nine and three-quarters, and I don't know enough to act my age. I'm a *single* woman. I don't know a thing about kissing men—"

"Oh, there you're wrong."

"Or anything about sex! I told you I didn't. If you have any idea that I would ever consider marriage, then you misunderstood me."

He nodded his head. "I surely did."

"Well, understand that I'm calling everything off."

"You're turning the pages back?"

She got to her feet. "I'm ripping them out."

He rose too, and picked up his crowbar and a hammer from the floor and a broom he had used to sweep up the small mess he had already made. "If I had a crystal ball, I bet I could see your friend on the telephone, calling you this morning."

"Grace?" she said. "What makes you think Grace called?"

He lifted his shoulders. "Intuition."

"I was sorting it out before she called."

He began putting his tools into the wooden crate. "Before I leave, let's go over to your house and have a little fig preserves and a slice of toast."

"You want to talk me out of it."

"I'd love to do that, but I don't think I can." He looked straight at her. "What I hope I can do is help you decide what you should do with your honeymoon cottage."

Anguish flooded her. "Maybe lightning will strike it."

"Maybe," he said, "it already has."

"What did you mean?" said Eleanor. "Over there. About lightning?"

He was buttering toast, a slice for her, one for himself. "You talked about foolishness. Maybe a bolt of foolishness has struck the cottage, doomed it, you might say, to go on falling apart." He spread figs on the toast. "Give it two or three years and you won't recognize it." He showed a sad smile. "Makes you want to cry, doesn't it?"

"You should be ashamed! Playing on my sensitivities."

"I'm helping you," he said, "to face the truth. When you've done that, you can reach a decision: to let the cottage fall down. Or to fix it up."

She drank tea without looking at him.

"Fact of the matter." He cleared his throat. "This is old ground you've already covered. You decided, remember? You gave me the go-ahead."

"That was before."

"Before the kiss, et cetera?" He ate a shiny section of orange from a plate she had arranged. "May I suggest to you that you tear out the kiss page and move on from there?"

"As if it never happened?"

"As if you dreamed it and woke up."

"Could *you* do that?"

"I can do what I have to."

Color rose in her cheeks. "Because that's how you've lived! That's the cold-blooded way you handled it when your wife left you."

He looked up from the napkin he was carefully folding. "We left each other. I went north. She went south and took the baby."

"The baby!" said Eleanor.

"Kit. Mary Katherine." He pushed back from the table. "We're getting off the subject."

Eleanor followed him to the drainboard. "You said you were married for only thirty minutes."

"It can happen in five, dear."

"My *meaning*," she said and drew herself up, "is that if you found out so quickly you didn't like each other, surely you would have abstained from—you would have stayed apart. You would have made certain not to bring a child into it."

He said, looking down at her, "The child came first."

Blood rushed to her cheeks.

"If that shocks you, I'm sorry."

"Of course it doesn't shock me." She gasped out the next bit. "Of course I'm shocked! It's shocking that you, you of all people, would have—that you wouldn't have—"

"Used better judgment?"

"That's it exactly! As steady as you've made me think you are—as thoughtful. As *kind*!" She began to cry.

He put his arms around her. "I think you didn't sleep the whole night long."

She hiccuped against him. "Haven't you ever had a night when you relived everything? Every damned word you said, every revelation? That business about the calendar. I never meant to tell anyone about the calendar."

"It's a brilliant business. But I'll keep it to myself."

She let him hold her until she could say without tears, "Have you ever looked at me, Abel? Really looked at me?"

He touched her hair. "I believe I've known you most of my life."

Eleanor wrote in her daybook:

June 28. Mother and Father, I have fallen in love. With an itinerant carpenter. His feet are huge. He can't play the violin. He moves around the country in a trailer no bigger than a sardine can. He's been in jail. He was a drinker. He was married once and has a child.

She lifted her pen from the page and stared out the window. *This is not the summer of my life. This is the middle of winter! What am I thinking of? What will become of me?*

She wrote again:

I have given him permission to renovate the cottage. Against all reason, I allowed him to kiss me. Your seventy-year-old daughter, only a few years younger than you were when you died, has taken up with a stranger. He doesn't seem like a stranger. He believes he has known me most of his life. I understand what he means. If I allowed myself to do so, I could believe that I have known him too, in a sealed-off place inside my mind that I wasn't aware existed, a place where I longed to love a man and be loved in return. I am totally unfit at this stage in my life for that kind of love, that kind of relationship; yet every new day the possibility excites me. I know that a possibility is all it is. Is more than it is. He has not proposed to me, of course, but he acts as if he thinks he has. He acts as if I have accepted him!

She paused once more to deal with a gray feeling creeping over her. An emptiness of heart. A banishment of hope. She uttered a moan and wrote again:

For my own protection I must adopt the same kind of distance from this situation as I did in the classroom when the need arose to maintain order. I must not forget that this love, as I have recklessly called it, will be over as quickly as it began. He will finish the cottage and drive off down the road. My current upheaval will become part of a dream—as he said once—from which I will awaken and be myself again, writing in this daybook about fig preserves and fire ants.

A stifled mewing replaced the moan.

When I fell in love,

she resumed unsteadily,

I mistook my feelings for symptoms of illness and put a plaster on my chest. If I were to marry him, how would I endure his first sight of my naked bosoms, my shrunken breasts, my flesh that has lost its youthful

*substance? Did I say he has a child? Yes, that too! Her
name is Kit. Mary Katherine. And somewhere he has
another wife. Another wife, as if I were his wife!
What would the town say to that? My former students
ogling me in the grocery store; Sissy pumping Grace
for details to spread around the community. It is un-
thinkable that I, Eleanor Bannister, would ever consider marriage.*

*So why am I thinking about it night and day?
Because it has become a game with me, a game to
while away the summer. In my senile madness I am
playing at being a bride.*

She returned to her daybook:

*Have I mentioned the groom's name? His name is
Abel Brown. If I were to marry him, I would be-
come—ridiculously, in the custom of the day—
Bannister-Brown, or, as he once joked, Brown-
Bannister.*

7

The days flew by as they never had before. Eleanor fell into bed at night and woke up fifteen minutes later to the morning sun shining in, a gladness filling her heart as she rose, eager to get on with her plans. There were so many things to do!

Breakfast first. A quick tidying up around the house, and then Abel's lunch to prepare. She couldn't wait each day to sit down with him at noon in the cottage kitchen to discuss the work. To look at him. To look at him looking at her.

Grace called when Eleanor was singing at her sink, slicing carrots for a stew she was making. "I don't suppose you'd be interested in going with me to the silver tea at the church."

"The silver tea! Is it time for that?"

"It's the same time every year, the first Monday in August."

"August already! It got here so quickly!" The tea, given basically to raise funds for the mission field, was the social highlight of the church year, a dressy occasion (some ladies even wore hats!). Ordinarily Eleanor anticipated it with pleasure. "Oh my, I do hate to miss it," she murmured, "but I can't go today." Today she had an urgent issue to discuss with Abel. "I'm sorry, Grace. I'll be too busy."

"You're busy every day," Grace said bitterly. "You can't think of anything except trotting back and forth from your house to that cottage. To your Mr. Brown! And don't think I don't know what's going on over there."

Eleanor laughed. "I'd like to hear what you think."

"You're gaga over that man."

"He's doing an excellent job of restoring my property. Why wouldn't I be over there supervising?"

"If it were old Pete Maloney doing the work, you wouldn't be 'supervising.' You'd stay out of his way till the end of the day. And if I know anything about men, your Mr. Brown would just as soon you'd stay away too, and let him tend to his business. And you ought to, Eleanor."

"Maybe you ought to tend to yours."

Grace gasped. "That's the rudest thing you have ever said to me!"

"I'm sorry, but there is no cause for you to be in a snit over something that does not involve you." A sniffling began in her ear. "Grace! Are you *crying*?"

"I was under the impression that we were friends."

"Of course we're friends. You're jealous, that's all! You're behaving like a child, and you should apologize to me for envying the pleasure I'm taking in this project!"

"Friends share things, Eleanor. They look after each other."

"If you are in some sort of jam and need looking after, you should say so. And you may come over here and help yourself to anything I have at any time, but I will not put up with hurt feelings and self-pity."

"If you should ever wish to talk to me again, you may call. Do not expect me to call you."

"Hell!" said Eleanor, banging down the receiver. The worst part about quarreling with Grace was the making-up scene: usually Grace, still weepy, brought over bread pudding or some such, and Eleanor was expected to scrape up something in return, most especially an apology, undeserved.

Eleanor shouted at the carrots on the drainboard, "I will spend my day any way I please. Whenever I choose I will 'trot over' with a hot lunch for Abel! It is entirely my affair!"

Except, of course, it was not an affair, no matter what Grace thought.

Eleanor brooded at the sink. What was it then? Was it love?

If it was love, was it going anywhere?

Did she want it to?

Whatever the answer to that was, she could not restrain herself (even for the sake of the silver tea) from going to the cottage at every opportunity. Every new nail that went into a board was a fascination. Even half a day away, and she missed something important. *She missed Abel*. When she closed her eyes she saw his face, smiling at her. She was constantly repeating to herself things he said. *Endearments*.

No, they were not endearments.

Yes, they were.

The telephone rang.

Grace's wavering voice came over the line. "I'm sorry, Eleanor. I'm having a spell with my hemorrhoids today, and I took it out on you."

"It's all right," said Eleanor. For some ridiculous reason she felt like crying herself. "I'm sorry you're in pain and that I added to it."

Grace laughed feebly. "You may be right, saying I'm jealous, but I miss your company."

"We'll go places again if you'll just be patient. This is a big undertaking for me, Grace. And expensive too." She gave a feeble laugh of her own. "I may have to get a job when it's all over."

"When it's all over, you'll be Mrs. Abel Brown."

"Grace, for heaven's sake!" But her voice trembled. If Grace could see how much Abel meant to her, then Abel could see it too. "I don't have time to discuss it now. I'm cutting up vegetables for a stew."

"So what should I tell the ladies at the church? You have never missed a silver tea. We depend on you to pour."

"You'll manage just fine. I have to hang up now, Grace, but you must pay attention to what everyone wears and what they say, so tomorrow you can give me a detailed report."

"Mr. Brown," said Eleanor, coming into the cottage kitchen, her chin barely visible above a box and a basket she carried, pressed to her chest.

"Miss Bannister, ma'am." He turned around, smiling. "Can I give you a hand?"

"I can manage, thank you. It's only the lunch." He was sweating. Too much, she thought, for a man his age. "While I'm laying it out, sit down and rest."

"In a minute," he said, going on with a window frame he was replacing.

Unfolding a camp table, Eleanor lifted a tea towel off the lunch basket and set out crackers, a water bottle, paper cups, and a covered bowl she handled carefully; then another filled with strawberries and two smaller bowls.

"Ready," she said. She stepped around the sink he had torn out days ago and left lying on the floor. An ancient thing that had rotted the timber of the wall behind it. Her advice at the time had been to put it in the yard and let the junkman take it.

"I'll get around to it," he had told her.

"Yes, but when?"

"It's on my Do List."

"Move it to your Do Now List before you fall over it."

"No danger of that."

"*I* might fall over it."

But there it still lay.

"Ready," she said again and watched him methodically putting aside his tools. "It's your turn, I believe, to sit on the crate. I'll take the sawhorse."

When he was settled at last, she smiled and handed him a plastic packet.

"Here's a soapy washcloth to clean your hands, and when you're done, please say the grace."

He followed her instructions and then bowed his head. "Thank you, God, for whatever this is."

"Stew," she said.

"For this excellent stew."

"Amen," said Eleanor, picking up the serving spoon.

But Abel went on, "And thank you, God, for the hands that prepared it."

Her hands. Eleanor's cheeks burned with shame. "Sorry," she murmured. "I thought you were finished."

"No matter," said Abel. He bit into a strawberry. "If God is God, he heard me anyway."

Eleanor blinked. *"If!"* she said. "You don't believe in God?"

"Oh yes, yes I do. If it weren't for God, I wouldn't be sitting here. I'd be somewhere in Montana." He smiled pleasantly. "Or Idaho."

Eleanor snapped, "God doesn't oversee every move we make!"

"No?" said Abel.

"Surely you don't think he does!"

"I think probably I do—which is not to say I'm always listening when the message comes through. Otherwise"—his smile broadened—"I'd have gotten here sooner."

She answered stiffly, "My idea of a personal God is not quite that personal." Without looking at him, she shook out her napkin. Linen. Her mother's. Or possibly her grandmother's. "Stew should be eaten while it's hot."

Abel's gaze moved beyond the steaming bowl she had put before him to the strawberries and to a little group of chocolate cookies—freshly baked, from the smell of them.

"It's nice of you, Miss El, fixing this meal for me. I thank you for it, and for all the other meals you've been bringing over."

Her voice warmed. "You're very welcome. I know if I don't fix something you'll skip lunch. A working man needs food in his stomach."

"I brought along an apple and a piece of hard cheese. Maybe you'd like a bite or two of that."

"No, thanks." She put down her spoon. "Actually," she said, "I'd like a little talk. If it won't disturb your digestion."

"About God? Or the fig tree again?"

"About you." She squeezed her fingers together tightly and forged ahead. "About your proposition, the proposal you made to live in this house while you worked on it." Every evening at five he drove off to his trailer, still located in Payne, and she didn't see him again until the next morning. "Does that still stand?"

He studied the silverware beside his plate. "Do we need all these utensils?"

"The fork is for the strawberries, the spoon for the stew."

"I see," he said. He speared a slice of carrot and chewed thoughtfully. "Miss El, beloved, we might need to go a little slower in this arrangement."

Alarm bells rang. "In what regard?"

"In the matter of moving. When I first brought it up, I had in mind buying a few sticks of secondhand furniture. A table and such. A comfortable bed. I thought I'd make a little nest here while the work went on." He drank slowly from his cup. "But it seems to me now it's more important for you to be comfortable, with your friends, you know, who might see a move on my part as too bold for an upstart fellow who just came to town."

"Is that all that's stopping you?" Her color came back. "People talking?"

"I've taken a few jabs at the gas station," he said. "And at the drugstore a lady from your church, Mrs. Sims or Simpson, asked a lot of questions like she's writing a book."

Mrs. Simpson, the former school superintendent's wife, had spoken to Eleanor too. "Just a word," she had said, "of friendly advice." And even Mr. Ashe, who swept out the church, had voiced a note of warning about fly-by-night men, his gaze all the while fixed on the Christ child in a stained-glass window.

"Small minds feed on gossip, Abel."

"Big ones too," he said. "It's a human condition. In a town the size of Grover people are bound to be curious." He winked across the table. "Especially about a figure as illustrious as you. I think it might suit better for me to stay on a while at the Family Campground."

"How long is a while?"

"Oh." He rubbed his chin, the same way, she noted, that her father had done when he pondered a decision.

"I have my own standing in Grover, Abel, and it doesn't depend on the likes of Mabel Simpson." Or old Mr. Ashe either, as kindly concerned as he appeared to be.

"In that case, then—" Abel looked past Eleanor toward the wall where the sink had been. "I guess I could move in here when I'm finished with the plumbing and we've turned on the water."

"Fine," said Eleanor. "I'll alert the water department this afternoon."

"No hurry. I still have the sink and a little pipe work to do in the bathroom."

"Here's another suggestion." Eleanor moved briskly to a plan from which she had shrunk earlier but which now possessed her. "Instead of renting out your trailer or paying to park it, move it here. There's plenty of room between the cottage and the thicket."

Abel frowned. "I'll need to think about that."

"It's the practical thing to do, Abel."

He glanced at her flushed face. "Maybe so. Maybe it is." He looked at the half-finished window she had called him away from. "If things don't work out, then I can hook the trailer back to the truck and move along."

Her heart stood still. "Things may not work out," she managed to say, "but that wasn't my thought."

"No," he said at once. "I can see it wasn't. More likely you were thinking how convenient it would be for me not to have to drive back and forth, to have at hand my cooking things and so on." His blue eyes twinkled. "Or maybe you thought I'd be homesick."

"Will you, do you think?" In the rush of relief, she missed his joke. "You've lived so long squeezed up in your sardine can." Then she saw all at once that Abel's stew was untouched. "Eat, Abel! Your stew is getting cold."

"There's so much going on here." But he applied himself to the stew, made appropriate compliments, and finished a second bowl.

"Now," he said, "I'm going to my truck and have a little nap."

Eleanor said eagerly, "Why don't we go get a bed and put it in here for naps? There are several nice ones in my attic. We could go over there now and bring one down."

"You and I?" he said.

"Why not?" said Eleanor.

"It's too hot, for one thing, and we'd probably both fall down the stairs, and the bed on top of us."

"I'm anxious, Abel, to get things going."

"Everything in its own time, that's the best policy."

"You're terribly holy, aren't you?"

"Holier than thou?" He gazed at her, laughing.

"Don't make fun of me!"

"No. No, I'm not doing that." He sat quietly while she busied herself, returning the dishes to her basket, and then he said, "A couple of things have occurred to me. I think I better say them before we go any further."

"It's a nuisance, isn't it, not to have water?"

"Come and sit down, Eleanor."

She came to the table. "First let me ask you, do you have indigestion? You look so—pained. If you do, Abel, I have Tums in my purse." She thought as she said it how easily she used his name now, how naturally she did so. And how happy it made her.

"I'm fine, Eleanor, but I want you to listen."

She resisted an urge to pat his hand and sat instead on the sawhorse. "Yes, I'm listening."

"Do you remember in the thicket when you told me you had to have your own room and that you got up in the night to take medicine?"

"Of course I remember. And you told me you watched television until two in the morning and got up to take walks."

"Yes," he said. "And I think we agreed that we've lived by ourselves most of our lives." His softened gaze rested on her lips, parted as she waited for him to go on. "What we were saying, my dear, was that we have our own way of doing things. Not that we couldn't change a few of them, but that we feel safe in the routines we've established for ourselves."

"Safe," she repeated. "I guess that's true."

He took a careful breath. "What I'm fixing to say is not to criticize you, or hurt you. Because I love you. I've already said that."

Her trusting look vanished. "Whatever you have to say, say it, Abel."

"I need to, but I hate to."

"You can do whatever you have to do. You said that yourself." She knew what was coming. She had known all along. She had written in her daybook,

Soon this will all be over.

But how swiftly it had happened! And how great the agony!

"Go ahead," she said in a hardened tone. "We can't sit here forever with these dirty dishes."

It seemed for a moment that he might laugh. Then he sobered again. "All right. Here's Number One: due to your kindness, you and I have had a number of pleasurable lunches. But I have to ask you, Eleanor, not to bring lunch over here again."

A slap would have had a gentler effect.

He went on quickly, "I'm sorry, Eleanor. But when I work, I eat lightly. An apple. Hard cheese. While I eat, I think. I figure out the job problems. I need solitude to do that. I plan my next step. And I rest in my truck. Even if I had a bed, I would rest in my truck. Because I've always done that. Because I want to."

He paused, studying her frozen look. "Eleanor?"

"Go on," she said.

"Maybe we'll skip this."

"I am waiting for Number Two."

"Number Two." He cleared his throat. "This may not seem like much to you, but somehow or other it's important to me."

"Get on with it, please."

"What I'm asking you to do, Miss El, is not to make a habit of popping in over here."

"Popping in!" Her tone wrote it hugely, in capital letters across a blackboard.

"I thought it best to mention it."

"Has it slipped your mind, Abel Brown, that this is my house? That I can pop in here whenever I choose?"

"Interruptions distract me, Eleanor. I work better and do a better job when I'm left alone."

Eleanor thought bitterly of Grace's words. "Is there a Number Three, sir?"

"Since you've asked, yes ma'am. I don't especially like it that you've started telling me when to eat, how to wash my hands, and where to sit." He tried another joke. "You're even saying *amen* for me."

"You outrageous man!" She shot up from the sawhorse. "I apologized for that!"

He put out a hand. "Oh, glory—calm down a minute. Listen to me. I'll say it in one sentence: I know what I need to do. I can make my own plans."

"That's two sentences, you booby! And you're a hypocrite too! Since the first day I met you, you've been making plans for me! You took over this roof when it had a hole in it! You planned the renovation and told me how to pay for it. You destroyed my steps without even asking— and look at my sink! It was your plan to tear out my sink! And that's how you'll leave it: ruined on the floor. I'll have to pay somebody to come in here and clean up your mess."

"I'll clean it up myself, but I'm going to finish my job first."

"You're a damn fool if you think I'll let you!"

"Oh, hell. You're taking this all wrong—or I said it wrong. I don't even know why I said it in the first place."

"I'm quite sure you do."

"Eleanor—"

"Don't you dare say you love me!"

"I do say it!"

She swept up everything but the half-full stew bowl and threw it in her basket. As she went out the door she said, "I've seen enough of you to last me forever."

The rest of the day Eleanor went around doing things with no purpose. Folding a damp dishtowel. Putting it in a drawer. Pulling it out again to throw it in the wastebasket. She watered an ivy still wet from the soaking she had given it after breakfast.

Finally, lost in her own kitchen, she fell down in a chair and wept for the stew she had left at the cottage. Wept for herself so happily chopping vegetables, making the stew. Wept because an unsummoned memory made real again a childhood morning when a nocturnal animal had ravaged her Easter nest.

She heard the truck leave. Not coming around the corner. Going away.

She blew her nose and set herself to washing the lunch dishes, singing in a cracked voice, "A Mighty Fortress Is Our God." The first line four or five times.

Then "Blessed Assurance," crying steadily. When the dishes were done, she went to her bedroom and brought out her daybook.

Bent over her desk, she scribbled across a page,

I have been flayed. My skin has been stripped off by cruel words and is lying where I left it, on the kitchen floor of the cottage, where I want never to go again. Mother and Father, a treacherous other self, lurking inside me all these years, unknown to me and unacknowledged, has shown itself and taken over my life, blinding me until today to the commonsense caution my friends have urged, filling me with impure desire, causing me to give my heart to an unworthy man who this morning crushed it and threw it back in my face. I am ruined. I cannot go on with the feelings stirred up by this wretched suppressed self, and I cannot again be who I was. If I weren't a Presbyterian, I would kill myself.

8

Eleanor lay abed until ten o'clock the next morning. Then she called Grace on her bed-side phone.

"I am ill unto death."

"Eleanor? Is that you?"

"Only partly me, Grace. The rest of me is a miserable, unwelcome being who has never been properly understood in all of her life and has chosen this hour to raise Billy Hell with me."

"You're out of your head! And seeing double! I'm coming right over."

"Yes, hurry. You know where the key is."

"No. Where is it?"

"You won't need it. I didn't lock up."

"You didn't lock up!"

In a minute Grace was there. Grace in a tizzy. "Eleanor, you're green! What have you done to yourself?"

"I have not done anything, only contemplated: poison," she moaned. "Sword. Natural gas."

"What on earth is wrong?"

Eleanor resituated a wet cloth over her closed eyes. "You've heard, haven't you, of being sick of a person? That is my illness."

"I'm calling the doctor!"

"I am sick of Mr. Brown. Do you know of a doctor who can cure that?"

"Mr. Brown!" Grace sank into a rocker and sat forward. "He attacked you, didn't he? Where? At the cottage?"

Eleanor groaned. "Why did I call you?"

"Because you want me to help you, and I want to, Eleanor! Tell me everything!"

"I will not tell you anything of what transpired between Mr. Brown and me except that it was verbal, not physical. And that it was insufferable and has put me to bed. I can't imagine I will ever get up again."

"Eleanor, what can I do?"

She removed the cloth from her eyes and waved a hand toward the desk. "Get a notebook and write down what I tell you. And then go over to my rent house, where Mr. Brown has been hammering for the last two hours, and read it to him. Read it in the same tone of voice you use on your yardman when he mutilates your shrubs."

Grace said gratefully, "That's more like you. But I need to know what Mr. Brown has done."

"He has behaved abominably, and you shouldn't be surprised. You were the one who warned me that he was not a decent man."

"I don't believe I said 'decent.'"

"Don't take anything back! It's all true. A single woman, you said, has to be careful. I apologize, Grace.

You were right about everything, except he doesn't want my house, he wants a slave, a mindless toady who does what he tells her, when, where, and how. Do you have the notebook?"

Grace scrabbled in a drawer. "Is this it?"

"That's my daybook! Put it down. Look under the dictionary."

Notebook found, Grace said, "Maybe you should eat something before we start."

"Eat! I would vomit on the bed."

"Oh, my. Well then, I'm ready, I suppose. But I could do a better job if I had an inkling of what the problem is."

"Mr. Brown and I had a disagreement that cannot be mended. Don't write that down! Write this: *You do not have my permission to work in my house.*"

"Slower, please."

"Where are you?"

"On 'permission.' The pen is skipping."

"Are you even trying to get this down? You have no idea of how I feel, Grace! Devastated. Kicked in the shins."

"Eleanor, you will feel one hundred percent better if you close your eyes and calmly picture the church parlor. Pink roses on the table in Ruth McCarthy's silver vase, the silver trays perfectly arranged with cheese straws, and those delicious little open-faced sandwiches, the olive-nut ones, you know, that Mercy Farnsworth always makes. She said to tell you—"

Eleanor sat up board-straight and broke in shrilly. "It is inconceivable to me that you could be so insensitive as to think I would give a hoot in hell about what went on at the silver tea! Or what Mercy Farnsworth says about anything!"

"You *asked* me to report every detail!"

"That was yesterday! Today I am beside myself! I am unable to think of anything except Abel Brown's treachery." Eleanor's voice cracked. "The time I've wasted putting up with that man!"

Grace closed the notebook. "We'll get back to this after you've had a little nap."

Eleanor fired up again. "Don't speak to me of naps! And if Mr. Brown is napping when you go over there, drag him out of his truck and read him this. Write it down, Grace! *Your inconsiderate hammering is disturbing ill persons in the neighborhood.*"

"Why is Mr. Brown hammering?"

"He's tearing up my kitchen, and I told him not to!"

"But if it needs tearing up—"

"All right, damnit! Don't write anything! Just go over there and tell him to get out!"

"Oh, I don't know—"

"Tell him I said so. And if he doesn't leave, I'm calling the law."

"We've never had anything like this on Tennessee Street."

"Mr. Brown is on Florida Street. When you get through, come back and describe his reaction.

"And one other thing," she called to Grace at the door. "If he says anything to you about popping in, you tell him to pop off permanently."

By the time Grace returned, Eleanor had regained some of her composure and was sitting in the living room, her father's violin in her lap, but she had not dressed or combed her hair or put on the touches of makeup she usually applied first thing in the morning. "I'm in here, Grace. How did it go?"

"Oh, fine. Just fine." A smiling Grace entered the room and held out a bouquet of zinnias in a turquoise vase. "Mr. Brown wanted to go to town and buy you flowers, but I said, 'Why not go over to my yard? I have flowers over there, and you can pick as many as you like. Eleanor loves zinnias.'"

"Did you tell him I was ill?"

"Well, no. I didn't have to. When I told him his hammering was disturbing ill persons, he guessed right away who it was. It was all I could do to keep him from coming over here that very instant."

"I hope you told him it would kill me if he did."

"I told him what you said, that you wanted him out."

"Did you say it forcefully?"

"I tried to, Eleanor, but he was so upset that you weren't feeling well." Grace looked around. "May I sit down?"

"What do you mean he was upset?"

"Well, actually, you may not understand this, but I believe I was wrong about Mr. Brown. He's an awfully nice man."

"A nice man! In my direst distress you would say that to me? Messengers, Grace, were stoned in Greece when they brought bad news!"

"What?"

"Sophocles said that. He said it for you, Grace! Three thousand years ago!"

"You're still overwrought, aren't you? Well, what I am trying to say to you is that Mr. Brown was distressed in the kindest way. Worried, Eleanor. He said maybe if he talked to you, and I said no, I didn't think so, that I had gotten the idea that you didn't want to see him ever again."

"What did he say to that?"

"Nothing for a minute. He just rubbed his chin and looked awfully sad."

"He puts on a good show."

"Oh, he was sincere. I'm convinced he was. He admitted he had said things to you—"

"—that he shouldn't have said!"

"He put it this way: 'I ran roughshod over her feelings, but not intentionally.' He said it tenderly, Eleanor. If you had been there, you would have believed him."

"That's it, don't you see! It's exactly what you said; he's a con man."

"I misspoke, Eleanor. I didn't know him then."

"And you don't know him now! You're just bowled over by him, the way I was. He's made a fool of both of us."

"I know something about men, Eleanor."

"You think so, just because you were married?"

"My Roger was a good man."

A *blockhead*, thought Eleanor. She had never understood how Grace could bear him.

"He was good, but he had tricky little ways that I learned to watch out for. I know what tricky men are like, and Mr. Brown isn't one of them."

"One experience doesn't make you a proper judge."

"Mr. Brown is charming. He's not tricky."

"You certainly formed a lot of opinions when you were presenting my case. Is he or is he not out of my house?"

"He's out. In fact, he's over at my house fixing a shutter. You know that wind we had? It's been dangling half off ever since. Abel said every time he's ridden by, he's wanted to stop and ask if he could fix it."

"Ask! I'm surprised *Abel* didn't tell you that you have forty other things he could easily do for you."

"Well, he did say that. Not forty, but four or five. The paint has chipped off the windowsills. He's going to see about that. And I need something done about my sidewalk. He knows about cement, how you have to use rods and tie them together to keep it from cracking."

"Did he close up my house, or am I going to have to go over there and shut it up myself? I'd better not find any of his tools in there."

"He was so nice when I came in. He had me sit down."

"On the sawhorse or the crate?"

"On a folding chair."

"A folding chair!"

"He went out to his truck and brought it in."

Eleanor got to her feet. "You'll have to leave now, Grace."

"You're exhausted, aren't you? Well, I need to go anyway. I want to get something together and offer Abel lunch."

"Lunch! You fool! Apples and hard cheese. That's what he lives on!"

"Try to rest a little. I'll call back later."

"You'll need to call somebody! You'll need a hospital if you get mixed up with Abel Brown!"

9

Eleanor went out in the early evening, still in her wrapper, and sat on her screened back porch. The locusts were finishing their day's droning. Sawing wood, her father had called it, but of course they weren't. They were drumming their abdomens. An auditory exhibition that sounded primarily sexual. She would be pleased, she thought, if they would shut up.

Otherwise, the evening was its soothing self: children calling across the block, a cool breeze from the south. The kind of evening she had loved as a girl, and loved still.

But now the gathering twilight provided the backdrop for a picture of her angry self flouncing out of the cottage yesterday, as out of control—as much a harridan—as she had ever been or ever thought of being. One minute in heaven, the next in hell. She sat limply and thought of Abel's harsh words and her own, more harsh than his, flying out of her mouth like hornets. Retaliation. If there was anything pagan, that was it. It never won battles, never set the stage for peace. And the impression she had left with Abel! She shuddered, thinking about it.

Abel, of course, had not been wounded, had in fact quickly availed himself of other employment and spent the afternoon working over Grace's windowsills, eating her cookies, and drinking her lemonade while Eleanor had watched through a crack in the drapes of her living room window. It might even have been beer Grace was dispensing! Roger's beer, part of the case he had brought home the day he died, leaving his teetotaling widow to rid herself of it whatever way she chose.

And there she was, for all Eleanor knew, palming it off on Abel! To jolly him up and make him forget the wrecked cottage kitchen, the jetsam and flotsam in which Eleanor all day had been literally drowning.

Eleanor closed her eyes, instantly repentant. None of this was Grace's fault. She, not Grace, had smothered Abel with unwelcome attentions and driven him from her life. She was responsible for the disarray in the cottage where she had forbidden him to go. The smashed dreams. Her stew molding on the table.

What should she do? Board up the place? Let dust collect on the beautiful new cabinets? Never go there again?

She sighed heavily, aware that the despair that had haunted her for months after her parents' deaths had come galloping back, teeth sharpened, taking hold again. All because she had let a man she had known only a few weeks so discombobulate her that she was bereaved all over again. What an insult to her parents! There could be no comparison between the excruciating loss of her loved ones and this—this minor upset that she had blown out of all proportion.

Nothing in her current distress could come anywhere near what she had endured the evening she received the news of her parents' accident. Still, there *were* similarities: the shock of life turning upside down. The forced recognition that even the most trusted relationships could in an instant be swept away.

She remembered sinking down in this very chair, her gardening gloves still on, too stunned to cry. Friends whispering, patting her shoulder, wiping their eyes, the good people of Grover who didn't know any more than she what to say or do.

After everyone had left—she had refused every offer to spend the night with her—she did finally weep. *Howl* was the word for it. She went into the thicket and wrapped her arms around the tree trunks. She cried out, *Where have you gone?* Hours later she found herself collapsed at the base of an old ash tree with barely enough strength to rise and go into the house.

Adding to her grief had been the stark contrast between the actual event and the way Eleanor had previously pictured her parents' passing. As they aged, she had, as a matter of self-defense, begun preparing herself for life without them, concentrating on practical matters with which she would have to deal. Making a list of possible pallbearers. Educating herself about the wiles of car dealers. Pondering her course of action if a hurricane struck.

Her father would go first; she was fairly certain of that. Every winter for years he'd had pneumonia. He was growing listless and forgetful. Her first responsibility after his death would be to help her mother through her grief, and then to interest her in new activities. Eleanor pictured herself as guardian, caretaker, stalwart daughter, seeing to business matters and house and yard care. After a time her mother would fall ill too, and Eleanor would accompany her to the hospital, hire nurses. She imagined herself strongly withstanding whatever occurred.

What she did not imagine—could never have imagined—was that they would die together on a sunny afternoon—*and take their love with them.*

The suddenness with which they vanished was stupefying. Eleanor was separating daylilies in the front flower bed as they drove away. She remembered waving in a rather irritated way as her mother called back, "Your supper is in the icebox if you want to eat early." Half an hour later both of them were dead.

No need for a day nurse.

No standing beside a hospital bed, holding Dad's hand.

In an instant they were gone. Physically gone.

In her days of looking ahead, she had reckoned with physical loss, but nothing had prepared her for the loss of their love. It was inconceivable that what she had taken as much for granted as breathing had disappeared as permanently as the sound of her mother's voice, the way her father sat, poring over a book.

Where was death's sting?

It was in the heart of her, in the hole left when death ripped out her parents' love.

She lost her bearings for a while.

She formed a mantra she recited on her way to school, while bathing, while eating: *I will get through this. I am still Eleanor Bannister. Nothing has happened that I cannot overcome.*

She saw later how close she had come to losing her mind. Every day required a different kind of strength, presented new battlements to climb. She healed, but so gradually that she had no presentiment of it until one evening—again on this porch and nearly a year into her solitary life—she sensed a sea change—a letting-go was what it was. Grief gave way to steadiness. Day by day she learned to rely on it.

But where was steadiness yesterday when Abel tore her to pieces?

Where was it when she raved at Grace?

And where now, when the hole gaped again where love had been—what she had so pitifully mistaken for love?

She closed her eyes and listened to the evening sounds of her neighborhood. To survive this calamity she must accept the end of the ridiculous dreams she had known (and not known) as false and hopeless and, harder still, face up to the truth that no possibility existed—had ever existed—for a young girl's kind of love to flourish at her time of life. And finally, unbearably, she must meet head-on the fact that in the eyes of the only man to whom she had ever opened her heart, she had shown herself to be less than perfect.

She brought out an already damp handkerchief and wiped her eyes. If these events had occurred in the life of someone else, she might have said, *I knew all along you were acting the fool.* She might have appreciated the irony in the way she and Abel were carrying on (she mostly) in the kitchen of the cottage that was designed to shelter happiness and had spawned instead a knock-down-drag-out!

But she was *not* someone else. Eleanor Bannister had behaved in a manner she had scorned in others. Throughout her teaching career, distraught mothers had confronted her, defending their offspring against injustices perpetrated by Miss Bannister in the classroom, reacting in the same irrational way she had reacted to Abel's criticism. She had become the mother of her own childishness, as if she were ten instead of on the brink of her eighth decade!

A rustling in the grass brought her forward in her chair, eyes opening wide, peering into the twilight. *If that Anderson dog is defecating on my lawn again—*

But instead of a dog, a voice, heartwarming, tentative, came out of the shadows: "Eleanor?"

"Abel?" Unbelievably he materialized, still in his work clothes, his cap in his hand.

"I looked for you in the thicket. Your bird was singing there earlier." He hesitated, one foot on the steps. "But if you'd rather not see me—"

"I do want to see you." She hid her handkerchief in her bosom. With an indescribable gladness all but choking her, she managed to say, "Come and sit down." And then almost normally, "Did you finish at Grace's?"

"I'd need a month to do that." He opened the screened door and paused again until Eleanor motioned him to a chair next to hers. "Grace has let things go." He sat uneasily. "The sidewalk, the gutters. I got a few windowsills painted today and replaced a board in her steps."

"Steps, apparently, are one of your specialties."

Abel's shoulders relaxed a little. "I nailed a shutter back too."

Eleanor had a fleeting remembrance of herself nearly naked in his truck. Then her father's violin tucked under his chin. "You made Grace your fan yesterday."

He chuckled softly. "If so, that's quite a switch."

"A purposely engineered switch, I would imagine."

Her wry tone brought a smile to his lips. "To tell you the truth, I did want a close-up look at Grace. All I'd ever seen was her back, scurrying into the garage."

"You saw her the day you came to town. She was getting out of her car when her niece Maggie was telling you that I might have a house on Florida Street for rent."

"Is that a fact? Grace was that woman?" He leaned back in his chair. "I like that. I like accidental happenings that overlap, that show up like signposts to keep you on track till you get where you need to go"—he glanced at Eleanor—"to the important happening that isn't accidental." He went on in a hopeful tone, "You sending me to Payne, that was the first signpost because of the connection with my relative by the name of Payne. You see how it works?"

"I see you believe it was the moving finger of God."

Abel laughed. "I'm glad your spirit isn't broken."

Eleanor bristled. "It would take more than a quarrel with you to break my spirit!"

"Good," he said calmly, "since that's all it was." He leaned toward her, his voice low and husky. "Just a quarrel, Eleanor, between two people set in their ways. One of them blind too. Blind to the sweet-heartedness of the other one, the good intentions. The love," he finished.

He went on before Eleanor could find her voice. "I apologize for that."

She turned away, fresh tears threatening. "I was at fault, Abel. I didn't understand what was back of what you were saying."

"I didn't understand it myself, how it must have sounded to you, until you told me off and sashayed out."

He shook his head. "I sat there like a block of wood until it finally came clear that what I had done to you was what I was trying to keep you from doing to me. And then when you did it back, I came down on you with all fours."

Eleanor brought out her handkerchief. "We won't talk about it."

"We have to thrash it out, Miss El, or it'll keep popping up."

"Or popping in."

He hung his head. "It was awful of me to say that."

"It was. It hurt me."

"I know. I'm sorry." He took her hand and squeezed it. "I thought I was defending something. My freedom, I guess it was. It came over me, sitting there in front of your good lunch, what a grip you have on me, and it scared me to death."

Eleanor stayed silent until a truck's roar on the bypass faded into the distance. "This afternoon," she said, facing him again, "I had time to think about everything, to better understand what upset you."

"Plain blame foolishness," Abel said.

"No, that wasn't it. It was something important that we both hold dear." Her voice strengthened. "People like us, Abel, elderly people living alone, have a powerful need to maintain our independence. It's what sees us through. Otherwise, how could we go on?"

"And I interfered with that, didn't I, showing up here when you were out in the dew picking your figs."

"You frightened me, barging into my life, taking it over with that roof business and all the rest when it's been my prerogative for years to make my own decisions. You upset everything, and then you walked out on me."

"You ran me off, remember?"

"Why wouldn't I? I thought you were a drifter. I couldn't afford to invest in you. It kept me up all night dealing with the fact that I already had, and I had no idea what would become of me."

Abel sighed. "Full of bluster, that's what I am. I do the most blustering when it looks like something fine might be slipping away from me. Can you forgive that, Eleanor?"

"In a way, Abel, it was your bluster that attracted me. Your take-over attitude, which I balked at at first—which I resented, actually. Then it became a plus in your column. It showed me you were a man who got things done. It imprinted you in my mind." She swallowed hard. "And in my heart."

He held fast to her hand. "So where are we now?"

"Sitting together on my porch." She paused at the wonder of it. "Would you like a dish of ice cream?"

He answered hoarsely, "I would like to take you in the house and show you how much I love you."

"With kisses?" She barely whispered.

"Kisses," he murmured, "will do for starters."

"That's all I'm ready for."

"Then that's all we'll do."

A surprising blast of cold air met them when Abel opened the kitchen door.

"Why, Miss El," he said, "you're air-conditioned!"

"For the past five years. At great cost, I might add."

"Why haven't I noticed the unit?"

"Because I hid it. In back, by the grape arbor. I hate the chunky look of it, and every time it comes on, it sounds like a junk wagon pulling into the drive."

"I can fix that."

"I seldom turn it on before the middle of August, but it was smothery this morning."

"After our spat," he said sympathetically.

"Spat," she repeated.

"It was more than that, wasn't it?"

She moved on quickly. "The house is more pleasant with the windows open in the early part of the summer."

He was here, standing in her kitchen. With kissing on his mind!

"Even in August I shut off the air conditioner at night and turn on the fan." She chattered on. "I can't stand to be cooped up, so I crack open a window next to my bed. *Bed!* she thought. *Of all times to mention sleeping arrangements!*

He moved closer and put a hand on her elbow. "You're not afraid? With the window open?"

"Grace is afraid. Grace is always twittering about men breaking in and stealing her grandmother's china."

Abel smiled. "You don't have any china?"

"I have a burglar alarm. A pair of heavy shoes I set on the sill as if I'm airing them. The burglar can't see there's a pie pan under them."

"Eleanor—" Abel laughed.

"Anyone trying to come in—"

"The china thief, for instance?"

"—will have to move the shoes. The pie pan will clatter to the floor and wake me up."

He straightened his face. "What will you do then?"

"Scream." She considered. "Or faint, perhaps." She might faint now. She crossed her hands on her chest to quiet her heart.

He encircled her with his arms. "You could always throw your book. You do keep a book on your nightstand, don't you?"

"The pie pans are a reasonable way to protect myself, Abel!"

"Yes. Yes, they are." He breathed against her temple. "I commend your ingenuity."

She tried turning away. "I'll dish up the ice cream."

"Let's eat it later."

He held her, trembling, against his chest.

"I'm frightened now," she said.

"I'm frightened too," he answered quietly.

"Why should you be?"

"I might be less than you hope I am. Not tender enough. Not the man of your dreams."

She buried her face in his shirt. "We'll kiss. That's all."

"We'll do whatever you want."

She felt her heart slowing. "I'd like to sit in the living room."

She went before him, switching on a lamp, sitting stiffly on the sofa beside her father's violin.

Abel picked it up. "Been playing this, have you?"

"I was holding it earlier."

"In your distress." He laid it carefully on the lamp table and sat beside her, stroking her wrists. "Were you thinking of what kind of man your father was? Wondering if he ever spoke to your mother the way I spoke to you?"

"I was holding it for comfort. The wood somehow. It warms when you touch it, and it eased me for a while." Then she burst out suddenly, "What I was thinking about was my girlhood. I never had boyfriends. The boys who took me to parties were urged by their mothers. They didn't ask me out afterward. And I didn't want them to."

"You were happier staying home with your parents."

"Much happier." Her brain throbbed with a need to reveal herself. "My father was imaginative, an excellent reader. He taught me how to play chess. We worked jigsaw puzzles, went for walks and to movies. And then later—" She paused to catch her breath. "Later I was busy looking out for them. When they were older."

"A full life, it sounds like."

"But not well rounded." She had never said that before, or admitted that she thought it. A second admission flew out of her mouth. "A girl at home doesn't have to worry about being a wallflower. Or about speechlessness and cold hands if a boy tries to talk to her." Eleanor gripped cold hands in her lap and licked dry lips.

"I wanted to be a girl boys would like, but I had no idea what that girl would say or do. I gave off an air of self-doubt; I scared boys away, my mother said. They had their own uncertainties, she said, and didn't need mine adding to them."

"Eleanor," he whispered, "you don't have to tell me this."

"I do. I do, Abel! But I don't know why."

"Because it's unfinished business." He kissed her forehead. "We're going to finish it now." Reaching around her, he turned off the lamp. "Those poor dummy boys will never know what they missed."

Eleanor closed her eyes. A Ferris wheel appeared, lifting her skyward. Her skirt flew free, the earth dropped away.

A long while later she murmured, "We're necking, aren't we?"

Abel said in her ear, "I believe we are."

"I'm necking in my wrapper."

"You're beautiful in your wrapper."

At some further point he put her gently from him. "We have to take a recess. Or hunt up a JP and get married tonight."

Eyes still closed, she said, "You did more than kiss me. You held my breasts in your hands."

"I did," he said.

"Did you find them wanting?"

"The occasion was wanting, or I would have shown you how I found them."

She straightened her clothes, the room blurring before her. "I'm glad, Abel Brown, that those dummy boys never touched me."

Rising unsteadily, she made her way down the hall.

In a while she came back, hair combed and powder on her nose. Abel was in the kitchen eating chocolate cookies from a jar on the drainboard.

"Am I glowing?" she asked, pausing in the doorway.

"Like a Christmas candle."

"Could I have another kiss before it goes out?"

Over ice cream she said, "You've kissed dozens of girls, haven't you?"

"And women too." Abel grinned. "I have a whole notebook full of nothing but their names."

"Were you ever in love?"

"Before now? No."

"Are we in love?"

"Do you think we are?"

She said seriously, "I'm in love with necking."

He put a spoonful of ice cream in her mouth. "You don't have a ham sandwich, do you, that I could add to these cookies?"

"You haven't eaten, Abel?"

"I didn't have much appetite, but I did stop at the pizza place for a cheese and pepperoni."

Eleanor shuddered. "I'd have indigestion all night if I ate that."

"I would have been better off myself eating at the Town Cafe." He gazed at her flushed face. "But they don't serve supper."

"When I was a girl," she confided, "the Town Cafe was the Confectionery. I went there with my friends after school. Before my father came home."

"Was your father a professional man?"

"He should have been a teacher. He had a scholarly bent. Loved history and the sciences. But he went into business. Evart's, his shop is called now. Down by the post office. Maybe you've seen it."

"Men's clothing." Abel flipped over his cap, lying on the table. "I bought this there. My old cap blew into the lake the first day I moved in. I almost moved on, but I went to Evart's instead." He winked. "Another signpost," he said.

"My father's sign said Bert's Haberdashery. Ethelbert was his name."

"*Ethel*bert?" he repeated. "That's a new one on me. I would have said *Ethel*-bert."

"People who didn't know him often did call him that." She gazed across at Abel. "Tell me about your father. What did he do?"

"He was an engineer. On a train. He used to take me with him sometimes and let me blow the whistle."

"When I was off at college, hearing a train whistle at night made me homesick."

"Where were you?"

"In Colorado. My father said the only school he would send me to was forty miles away. In San Marcos. My own choice was Rice Institute in Houston. But my mother's idea was that they were both too nearby. I'd be on the bus every weekend coming home, which was what my father wanted. But my mother was right. I did need to get away, so I went to Denver, to a women's college there. I finished in three years." She smiled. "Then I came home with my sheepskin, and I've been here ever since."

"Any regrets?" Abel asked.

Eleanor moved a salt shaker in a circle on the tabletop. "It was a failure of imagination, my returning. When I left college, I left the college girl there. Once I was home, I couldn't picture myself having any other identity except as my parents' daughter, here in this town. In this house, actually."

"So you never lived in the honeymoon cottage?"

"No. It was a fantasy I had when I was a girl, to live there as my parents had, but they were settled in this house by the time I was born."

She lifted her chin, mildly defiant. "It was my decision to stay here. I'm glad for the years I had with my parents. It was a different kind of life, of course, than I might have had otherwise, but it was a good life, a happy life. We enjoyed each other. I never wasted my time mooning over what I might have missed. Others have missed what I had. In the long run, I expect they and I have lived pretty much as we wanted to."

Abel studied her silently.

"What are you thinking?"

"I was wondering when your parents died."

"Years ago. And suddenly. Both of them together. My father had a stroke driving the car." She fixed a tender gaze on Abel. "You know everything about Eleanor Bannister, and I know nothing about you, about the son of the train engineer. Were you a happy boy?"

"Reasonably so." Abel shifted in his chair. "My mother died when I was fourteen. An infection from a ruptured gall bladder. We rattled around after that, with aunts coming in, that kind of thing. When I was old enough, I joined the army."

"Of course. You were in the war. Where?" asked Eleanor.

"All over western Europe."

"How long were you there?"

"Until it was over."

"And you escaped being wounded?"

"I was lucky." He took up the salt shaker Eleanor had abandoned. "I had a younger brother born a few years before my mother died. Jim. He wasn't lucky. He died in Korea. In that war."

"I'm sorry." She took his hand, caressing his thick fingers.

"Jim left behind a responsibility when he went overseas. A woman. Pregnant. He left before he knew. And then he died."

After a moment Eleanor found her voice. "What happened to the woman?"

"I married her," said Abel. "And she gave birth to Mary Katherine. To Kit, who has believed all her life that I'm her father."

10

Eleanor in her gown sat at her desk and wrote,

I am a woman old enough to be lying down dying and yet have no more wisdom than a bald-headed cat! The most pitiful part is I have thought myself wise, thought highly of how I have handled my life, of the way I have managed for myself in a dignified manner and made a place of respect for myself in the community. But circumstances have made plain to me today that I have done nothing since you died, Mother and Father, but concern myself with myself! In bed at nine o'clock. To the library every Friday, so wrapped up in my sacred routine I might as well be one of those mummies in the British Museum for all the good I have been to anyone else.

Abel, on the other hand (I have spoken to you of Abel), early in his life when he should have been looking for a woman to fall in love with (praise God, he didn't find one!), married a woman he didn't even know who was carrying his dead brother's child and gave that child the name she would have had if his brother had lived.

Think of it, dear parents! That kind of sacrifice. That kind of nobility. You would expect your daughter, would you not, to recognize the extraordinary goodness in such a man? I did fall in love with him (at the ridiculous age of sixty-nine), so I must have recognized something, but then I turned on him the minute he stood up to me. I took to my bed like a deranged baby, dramatizing my hurts way out of proportion, making myself sick.

How is it possible that without even knowing it, I have grown from being your beloved child into a selfish, silly woman? The kind of woman I myself cannot abide. In the full light of truth I have seen my weaknesses. I have confronted my shortcomings. I have contrasted who I am with who I thought I was, and I see I have learned nothing from the hundreds of books I have checked out of the Payne Public Library. Nothing from the calamitous lives of the characters who peopled them. Instead, I have been Miss Eleanor Bannister, encased in her house on Tennessee Street, oblivious to life passing her by. Seventy years of it!

The miracle is that in spite of all my failings, Abel has fallen in love with me! He has seen in me qualities I do not possess, that will never be mine except in his eyes. He forgives me everything by denying there is anything to forgive.

How glorious—and how daunting!—my life has become.

Eleanor hummed as she washed her breakfast dishes the next morning, but when Abel's truck pulled into the drive, the tune she was striving for died in her throat. *Something is the matter!*

She hurried to the door. "What is it, Abel?"

"Do you mean what am I doing here while you're still in your wrapper?"

"I am fully dressed!"

"Alas, so you are." He gave her a quick kiss, a married couple's peck, which eased her fear that he had come out of regret for the evening just passed. Or worse, that he had come to apologize for it, which she couldn't have borne after lying half awake all night, glorying in the turn her life had taken.

"I'll get you a cup of tea."

"No tea," he said. "We're going for a ride in the country."

"Why?" she asked.

"Because it's a beautiful day. Because the crops are coming in. The milo harvest is about over, and they're starting to cut rice."

"Oh!" she exclaimed. "I've forgotten David Witcher!"

"Who?"

"A rice-farmer friend. I stopped one day on my way home from Payne to look at his field. We had a little chat, and he invited me out to see his crop at harvest time."

"An old widower, I suppose, with bread he wants you to bake and a nice old farmhouse he'd like to shut you up in."

Eleanor laughed, pleased at this spark of jealousy. "He's a former student. A pupil, actually." She bustled back to the sink. "There's a difference, you know."

"What kind of difference?"

"A student, Abel, is interested in learning. A pupil is only interested in getting out of school."

"Ah, yes. I pupiled through school for eleven years. Almost twelve." He clapped his hands together. "Take your apron off, Susie, time's a-wasting. Mr. Taylor says the choice hour to view the countryside in August is as soon after six in the morning as you can get there."

Eleanor dried her hands. "Who is Mr. Taylor?"

Abel's eyes twinkled. "An old widower *I* know. His son Dudley works at Evart's."

"Oh, yes." She had never met Mr. Taylor, but she knew he had come to Grover to live near his son after his second wife died. Dudley had grown up living with his stepfather, she remembered, a rough-talking man, but Dudley had turned into a fine man.

"Bill and I eat supper together now and then," Abel went on. "He's on his own like I am. A nice kind of fellow."

Eleanor said abruptly, "What about the cottage? You didn't work yesterday."

"I had orders not to." He softened his words with a comical lift of his eyebrows. "Now put on your shoes, or whatever you have to do, and let's get going."

For the first little while Eleanor was uncomfortable, not from bouncing over gravel roads in Abel's truck but from the way the day had veered from her plans to balance her checkbook, bake something for Grace to make up for yesterday, and, if she had time, scrub the tiles on her drainboard.

The morning, however, was not to be denied the admiration due its cloudless sky and the rare August breeze blowing her hair all over her head in a wanton way she wished Abel would stop whistling long enough to notice.

"Slow down," she said when they came up on the highway. "That's David's field there. One of six he farms. Look at it, Abel." He pulled alongside the field. "Isn't it beautiful, that waving grain? But shouldn't he be cutting it? Before the blackbirds get it," she added, proudly knowledgeable.

Abel shrugged. "Still too much moisture in it, I suspect."

"It hasn't rained in ages!"

Abel patted her hand. "*Natural* moisture. From the growing process."

"Do you have to know everything?" Eleanor said.

"Even pupils," he chided, "pick up a few things."

He had stopped the truck in almost the same spot where Eleanor had paused weeks ago to ponder her troublesome involvement with Abel. Now, on this glorious morning, she had no problems, and Abel's expression seemed to say he had none either.

She sighed contentedly. "I could never be a farmer. Too much uncertainty."

"Hard work too." Abel closed his fingers over hers. "I tried it once for part of a summer. Worst damn job I ever had. Grit in my mouth all day long, and every five minutes I was gulping water."

Eleanor teased, "Is that why we're out here, so you can congratulate yourself on quitting when you did?"

"I didn't quit," Abel admitted. "I got fired for lying down between the rows, checking out hawks diving at field mice."

"How old were you then?

"Old enough to know better. My father raised Cain with me when my uncle told him what a lazy son he had."

"You weren't really lazy."

"Oh, really I was." He smiled in a pleased way. "I still am when the spirit moves me. Like today," he added.

Eleanor thought, *A man roaming over the country all his life can be as idle as he pleases with no father to raise Cain. Or a wife.*

She turned back to the window, trying to ignore a chilly feeling that in spite of the heat had crawled up her spine. "Have you noticed the scissortails?" She pointed out a pearly-gray bird rising from a fencepost, its exotic scissor-like tail streaming behind it and a delicate salmon color lining its underwings and the sides of its pale breast.

"Up from Mexico," she said. "Spending the summer. I've counted eight so far, some of them with fledglings. They used to nest in town, on top of the light poles, but the squirrels got their eggs and they don't come anymore."

Abel pointed out another bird. "What's that little fellow further down?"

"A dickcissel," she said promptly. "A miniature meadowlark."

"Rarely seen in town, I guess."

"Rarely seen here at all, except at this time of year and into the fall."

"Did your father teach you about birds?"

"I taught myself, but he gave me a field guide when he saw I was interested." She glanced ahead. "Abel, where are you going?"

He had guided the truck away from the field onto a lane leading to a creek.

"Why are we going down here? To neck?" Her light tone belied the reluctance she felt at this unexpected turn of events.

"Why not?" said Abel. "You're in love with necking."

"Not in a public place! Not in broad daylight!"

He stopped the truck under a cottonwood tree. "We could drive around a while and come back at sundown."

She saw that he was teasing and leaned limply against him. "I should make you take me home."

"I will if you want me to. Or," he said, "we can cool off a bit and listen to the water."

"We should have brought a picnic lunch."

"How about an apple and a piece of hard cheese?"

She pinched his arm. "I used to do that to boys at school when they forgot their manners."

Abel laughed. "You couldn't do it now. You'd go to the penitentiary for abusing children."

"I know," she said ruefully. "I left the profession just in time."

They sat quietly, listening to the whisper of the cottonwood leaves, the little lapping noises the creek made.

"Like hiccups," she said.

He nuzzled her cheek. "Maybe just one kiss? While no one's around?"

"Abel, no."

"Maybe two little fast ones? We can hear a car coming half a mile down the road."

"I don't think we should."

His lips moved on her mouth. "You can tell me why later."

No cars passed.

The sun shifted through the tree limbs. Eleanor said softly, "Did you sleep well last night?"

Abel sighed. "Hardly at all. When I got back to the trailer, Kit called."

She glanced at him, surprised. "You have a telephone in the trailer?"

"I have one of those little things you carry around. Half the time it cuts out what you're trying to hear, but I heard enough to wish I hadn't answered it."

"Why? What was wrong?"

"Something is always wrong when Kit calls."

Eleanor waited for him to go on.

"My daughter is married to a good fellow, Eleanor. Don Florentino. But I'm sorry to say he's mostly good for nothing. He's left home again on one of his periodic jaunts to God knows where. Just when I'd begun to think he'd gotten over that foolishness, he's taken off again."

Eleanor said without thinking, "Something like you."

Abel turned his head sharply. "I never had a family depending on me."

"You had Kit and her mother."

"I was divorced from her mother when Kit was a baby. She never knew what it was like to have a father around. Abby does."

"Abby?"

"Kit's daughter, hers and Don's."

"You have a granddaughter?" Eleanor blinked. "Do you ever see her?"

"Two or three times a year. We write letters. The first time Don took off, they lived with me for four months."

"In your trailer?"

"Yes. It was crowded as the devil, but it worked out all right, two grown people and a three-year-old. But it wouldn't work now, though Kit wants it to. I told her she needs to stay where she is. Abby's ten and doesn't need to be yanked around the country, especially so soon after her father's deserted her."

"This is a terrible tale, Abel!"

"And sadly, not a new one. But at least this time they have their rent paid a month in advance. By the time it's due again Don could be back—if he's finished running through the money he cleaned out of their checking account."

"Does Kit have a job?"

"She quit a good one a couple of years ago when it looked like Don was going to be around for a while. Now she can't get it back, and she won't take anything that pays less than she made."

"That's foolish, Abel!"

"Of course it is. I told her to take whatever work she can find while she looks around, but Kit's not famous for taking reasonable advice. I wouldn't be surprised if she showed up here tomorrow."

"Can't her mother help?"

"Her mother died a while back, but she wasn't much good with practical matters. If Jim had lived, they wouldn't have lasted five minutes together."

Abel stared out at the creek, glinting in the sunlight. "Another thing. I've given Kit bonds for every birthday. Thirty-seven. Now she's talking about cashing them in, even though she knows they're for Abby's education."

"Abby's only ten. Kit thinks she'll have years to make it up."

"The years will go by, and she won't have anything. I hope Don's gone for good this time so she'll face the fact that she has to grow up if Abby is going to."

They sat, saying nothing, Eleanor holding his hand, smoothing the hair on his wrist. *A hairy man. Why was that thrilling?*

In a while Abel said, "I passed over your comment about Don and me being something alike."

"That was a thoughtless thing to say, Abel. From what you've told me, you're nothing like Don."

"In a way I am. I've never stuck around anywhere for long. I was always moving in the army, and after I came home I kept up that pattern, at loose ends kind of, thinking the next place would be it, I'd settle down." He locked his fingers in hers. "You sized me up pretty well the first time you saw me. A drifter, you said."

Her cheeks burned.

"Probably somewhere in your mind you're still thinking that. And you have good reason to. I haven't done anything to prove that I'm not."

"You're still here," she said in a small voice.

"Which may be some kind of miracle. Kit's roving father hasn't stayed put since the day she was born, not because I'm shiftless or irresponsible. I've never left a place because I owed money or because the work was boring or too hard." He smiled. "Except for the time I was watching those hawks."

Eleanor was too unsettled to smile back. "What drives you, Abel, from one place to another?"

"A feeling I get."

"A feeling! Restlessness?"

"It's more than that. It's like a big hand shoving me. When it strikes, I'm a goner. I have to pack up and move down the road."

Thoroughly chilled now, Eleanor said, "Then it's a matter of self-control."

"Or the lack of it. Isn't that what you mean?"

She glanced away from his steady gaze. "When I asked you why you were in Grover, you said you saw the lake and stopped." She forced herself to look back at him. "Is that really how it happened?" *On a whim he had changed her life.*

Withering inside, she watched him silently rubbing his chin as her father had done. It was a mistake to have fallen in love with him, to have fallen so far out of her own realm that she had no place to go, neither forward nor backward.

"I can tell you this," he said finally. "The first time I drove up Florida Street and saw the honeymoon cottage and the state it was in, something took hold of me that wasn't restlessness. The next morning as early as I could I went back to look at it, and I could no more stop myself from turning into that driveway and climbing up on the roof than an egg could keep from hatching."

"It was the carpenter in you," she said numbly. *I have to steel myself. I will start now, feeling nothing.*

He put his arms around her, his cheek against hers. "I haven't talked so much in I don't know when. Are you worn out with me?"

"Truthfully, Abel, I don't know what I am."

"Hungry maybe?"

"Maybe," she said.

"We'll drive over to the deli. We're halfway there if I can find the shortcut back to the highway."

11

Sitting in the Payne Deli that day, looking across the table at Abel enjoying a ham sandwich, it occurred to Eleanor that he was like a man with a terminal disease. He had grown so used to it that he could discuss it as if it were as ordinary as the weather and have no idea how shocked and devastated his listener was.

"You aren't eating."

"I'm going to." She picked up her chicken sandwich and set it down again.

"What are you thinking?"

Did he imagine she had anything on her mind except that he might pick up and go at any minute? "I was thinking about the cottage," she lied. He deserved a lie after the blow he had dealt her!

"I meant to tell you this morning and I got off the track." He drank from his tea glass. "I'm moving the trailer today."

There! There was the reason for this "country outing." "Where are you taking it?"

"Eleanor?" He frowned. "I'm taking it to the cottage. Unless you've changed your mind."

"Oh! To the cottage! To the cottage, of course." He meant to put his trailer in her yard as she had asked him to! He wasn't leaving. Not today or tomorrow. Maybe never. Could she hope for that?

Abel said, puzzled, "Are you sure it's all right, Eleanor?"

"It was my idea." But already she was remembering that Abel knew as little about his future as she did. The big hand shoving him made the decisions.

She pushed her plate away. "I'm not hungry, Abel."

He studied her face. "Miss El, I've upset you. I talked too much about my problems."

"I want to know about your problems. I want to help you if I can." She put several fingers to her temple. "But right now I think I'm having a stroke."

He regarded her tenderly. "You're tired and you're hot. Maybe ice cream will help."

He came back with a dish of vanilla and sat down again. In a low, comforting tone, he said, "This business with Kit will come right somehow. It always has. And that other thing—it may never happen again. I'll probably be hanging around Grover when I'm a hundred and five."

Eleanor said, "I'll be gone by then. No one in my family ever lives past ninety."

On the way home she asked him petulantly, "Why were you so sure I wasn't having a stroke? I could have been, you know. Ice cream might have been the worst thing you could give me."

"I guess I caught on that the details of my life are shocking to you. That's how you looked. Shocked," he said. "You needed reassurance, not a doctor."

Eleanor tightened her lips. "If I ever tell you again I am having a stroke, call one, please. And don't delay."

For a week after their ride in the country, Eleanor held herself in check when she thought about Abel. A dozen times a day she looked from her kitchen window through the thicket to where he had parked his trailer, but she forbade herself to think about him as someone she had once loved, and she went to the cottage only briefly to look at his work.

"I see you've gotten rid of that sink," she said one evening.

"It's in the truck. I'm thinking of recycling it."

You'll sell it, she thought, *to some poor person who won't know any better than to think it's a bargain.*

She commented on the progress he was making in one of the bedrooms. She walked around for a few minutes, and then she went home without asking him to supper. Once when he invited her to eat with him, she declined abruptly. She wanted to read, she said.

"You still have to eat."

"I ate a late lunch."

He looked at her sadly. "Suit yourself."

She wrote in her daybook:

I have no choice but to regard him as a person totally apart from myself. I can have no interest in him except as my carpenter. If he leaves the job before it's finished, I will shut up the cottage. Or set fire to it, after all.

Grace came over. "Things have gone wrong, haven't they?"

"I believe my initial assessment of Mr. Brown was right."

"You don't look well."

"Because I'm seventy years old! I'm not supposed to look well."

"You've looked bad for a week. And Abel," she said, "looks worse than you do."

"Of course. He's older."

That night she slept on the living room couch. Another night she set the metronome ticking on top of the piano. She turned her television on and turned it off. She took off her nightgown and lay down naked. At dawn she got up, dressed, and got the paper, feeling as raw as if she were burned.

In the house again, she glanced by habit toward the cottage and saw the spot empty where Abel parked his truck. *Gone.*

He was gone!

"I don't care!" she gasped and sank into a chair. "I'm glad it's finally happened!" The newspaper, face up on the table, showed a picture of a woman with a snake draped around her. "And you, you fool!" Eleanor raged at the grinning face. "Do you think you're invulnerable? That nothing can hurt you?" Then she laid her head on the kitchen table and cried into a dishtowel until she went to sleep.

He was away all day and all night. She got up twice to see. On the afternoon of the second day, she heard the truck door slam, and when she hurried to the window she saw him walking toward the trailer with a grocery bag in his arms.

Whistling, goddamnit.

She went over at once, barely knocking before she entered. "Where have you been?"

Abel paused, setting down a can of vegetable soup. "Out of town," he said. "I'm surprised you missed me."

"I didn't *miss* you! But I certainly was aware that you weren't working. You are in my employ, and I have a right to know when you are taking the day off. Two days! And a night!"

"I don't work at night," he remarked steadily. "And I am not in your employ. I'm not on your payroll."

"I am giving you free this place to park your trailer!"

"If you're keeping books, you may want to compare the hours I've worked free to the cost of parking fees. You'd come out ahead. Way ahead."

"You have the gall to throw that in my face? When you're the one who offered free labor?"

"Because I wanted this house to be all it can be."

"And now you don't want it! You'll loaf around here until your mysterious spirit orders you to go!" Her voice broke. "And you'll be gone."

He walked over to her.

"Don't touch me!"

He put his arms around her. "Except for the loafing, what you say may happen. I don't know that I won't pull up stakes one day."

"Like your son-in-law." She wept.

"You have my heart, Eleanor, whatever happens."

"You've been leading me on since the first time you kissed me. You figured up the months until we could marry!"

"I was dreaming, Eleanor, of staying with you forever. I'm still dreaming, but I can't promise you anything."

She went home after that. She told him not to walk with her.

Two endless days passed. She refused even to glance out her kitchen window toward the cottage. Her heart hung in her chest like a sluggish lump of meat. She saw herself in a mirror, a wild-eyed wraith who hadn't combed her hair or washed her face. Had she eaten? She didn't know. That evening she huddled in her father's chair, opening the Bible to vivid descriptions of God's wrath against the Israelites. She had no pity for them. She only pitied herself, a righteous woman led astray by a feckless man she shouldn't have given the time of day.

At some point that night, Abel picked a bouquet of flowers from Grace's yard and laid it on the steps.

He mowed her lawn the next day. She heard him hammering.

Like water dripping on a stone, the passing hours wore away the strain between them.

Eleanor wrote a note and put it in his truck: *I'm cooking a pot roast. It's too big for me to eat by myself.*

After supper he asked, "Can you help me wallpaper the bathroom tomorrow?"

Yes, she said, and she would like to iron his shirts. She missed ironing her father's.

They went to a movie and left in the middle of it to go home and neck.

12

Summer passed into fall. The night skies were full of geese, and Eleanor had run her heater for three mornings straight. She was wearing her warmest sweater when Cleo knocked at the back door before eight o'clock.

Skinny Cleo Carter. Cleo Carter Block since she had married Freddy twenty years ago. Or was it forty? Enough time anyway for her to have five children and Freddy to run off and come back and run off again.

"It's a fine bird-singy morning, ain't it, Miz Bannister?"

"*Isn't* it, Cleo."

Cleo laughed, the poor wrinkled thing. "You don't never give up, do you, Miz Bannister? When you was first teaching down in the grades, you was harping on *ain't,* and here I'm old and it still hadn't took."

"Well, maybe I failed in the grammar department, but you always did well in geography, Cleo."

"In geography I was working with a clean slate. I hadn't never heard of Alabamer and Rhode Isle or any of them other states till you drawed that map on the board and said fill it in or forget about passing on to the sixth."

She added happily, "I sure had me a good time learning about them states. Specially Delerware. Painted it red on all my maps. You remember that, don'tcha? Remember how I loved Delerware Punch?"

"Yes, well, your maps were beautiful. Painstakingly made, Cleo. Clean and neat, the way you clean houses."

Cleo said, pleased, "I still got some of my maps. I sure hated it when you moved up to high school. I knowed I'd never see you after that."

"We see each other, Cleo."

"It ain't the same, Miz Bannister."

"No. No, it isn't. Will you come in for a minute? I was having my tea."

"Yes'm, I will. I need to ask you something."

They stepped into the warm kitchen, and Cleo sat gratefully at the table. "Been up all night with Harley Rae's girl. Got the croup, I guess, and Harley Rae, she's working 'leven to seven at the drive-in store and trying to go to school."

"Harley Rae? She's going to college?" Eleanor remembered a scruffy young girl, fingernails painted green, groaning over *Macbeth*. "Well, I think that's wonderful!"

"Thirty-five years old and she finally got some sense."

"She has a husband, I believe?"

"Dudley. Yes'm."

"Dudley Taylor. Still at Evart's, isn't he?"

Cleo nodded. "Still sweeping up and taking out the trash. But he's learning 'lectronics. When he gets it straight, Harley Rae says he's gonna make lotsa money. Anyways, he don't drink. Ain't that God's blessing! And he's steady too."

Eleanor brought orange juice to the table, and warm cinnamon rolls.

"Just looky here!" Cleo selected the largest one. "I betcha these come from over at Payne." She cocked her head sideways. "I seen you with your feller over at Payne."

"Cleo—"

"It's *nice*, Miz Bannister! I always did hate it you never found you a sweetie."

"Mr. Brown is a carpenter. He is renovating my rent house."

"He's your boyfriend too. I knowed it when I saw how you looked at each other."

Eleanor tried to catch a calming breath. "What is the question you came to ask?"

"I was wondering when you and him is going to get married." Cleo's cackles filled the kitchen. "I'm joking, Miz Bannister." Still, she couldn't resist adding, "But if you'd like to tell me, I'd sure like to know!"

Eleanor said stiffly, "You are overstepping, Cleo."

"I'm sorry, ma'am." Cleo straightened her face. "What I really come to ask was if you had any dresses you don't wear no more."

"*I have displaced the mirth*—" Eleanor thought with regret. *And on a bird-singy morning*. "Oh, Cleo, any dress of mine would swallow you."

"They ain't for me. They're for Harley Rae. She's having a sale."

"How enterprising. A garage sale?"

"We don't have no garage. She's having it on the side-walk if it ain't raining Saturday. In front of Evart's. Mr. Tom said she could."

"Mr. Tom is a kind man." Eleanor ached to be a kind woman. "I imagine he thinks highly of Dudley."

"Oh yes, ma'am, he does. Your Mr. Brown does too. Said he might hire Dudley and his dad to help him finish up."

"Finish up my cottage? It's way too soon to be thinking of that!"

"Just a few more weeks is what he said."

Weeks! thought Eleanor. "I'm sure he meant months."

"I guess I coulda heard wrong." Cleo drained her juice glass and rose to go. "Anyways, if you run across a dress or two, I'd be obliged if you'd call me. We got a phone now so Harley Rae can take orders for the cakes she makes."

"She's baking too?"

"She's working real hard to gather up money for the next school term."

Remorse bulldozed Eleanor into saying, "If you could find the time, Cleo, in the next several days, you could come help me clean closets. I've been needing to do that, and we can surely find something for the sidewalk sale."

"Oh, Miz Bannister!"

Eleanor braced herself against an impending hug that didn't materialize. "Could we start right now?" Cleo asked. "I don't have no jobs till next Monday morning."

"Well, I suppose we could—if you aren't too tired from being up all night."

"I ain't tired at all. That cinnamon roll rested me. Do you know who does the baking over there?"

"Where?" said Eleanor with a sigh.

"At the deli in Payne. Lizzie Porch. You remember her, had moles on her cheeks and that funny walk? She's had the moles took off, but she waddles worse than ever since she got her bunions."

"Come along," said Eleanor, pointing Cleo toward the hall.

They began work in a closet at the back of the house where Eleanor had stored her parents' clothes. Cleo was courteous, but it was soon clear that she was disappointed. "These is beautiful things you're hauling out, Miz Bannister. But not something you'd be likely to see walking around downtown."

"No, certainly not. Those two dresses you're holding are Bemberg sheers made of a very fine fabric, from Europe, I believe."

"When was that?" asked Cleo.

"Oh, in the '30s. Before World War II."

"That's kind of what I mean. Ain't nobody going to buy a dress as old as that. Least not in front of Evart's on Saturday morning."

Eleanor stared. "Time gets away, doesn't it?"

"Shall I hang 'em back up?"

"I'll do it later." Eleanor took the dresses and laid them across a chest. How horrid anyway, her mother's lovely things displayed on Main Street with strangers' hands raking through them. "They belong in a museum."

"Yes'm," said Cleo. "Kind of like what you got here. But I don't expect many folks sees 'em."

"No one sees them."

"I can run the vackum through there if you want me to. Or I could dust," Cleo said. "The shelves and all."

"No, we'll go on. I have another closet where there might be things suitable for Harley's sale." She led the way down the hall—*her hall,* but Cleo seemed in possession of it, pausing to eye each framed face staring down from the walls. "Is these your grandpas and such?"

"My ancestors, yes."

At the door of Eleanor's bedroom, Cleo halted. "And this is where you sleep!"

As if I were George Washington! Eleanor thought. What a dreadful day! And what a foolish mistake, to expose everything that was private and personal to Cleo's gaze. "What you see in my house," she warned, "you must not speak of to other people."

"Oh, no'm! I won't."

At once she felt ridiculous. It was not as if she were concealing dark secrets or even anything especially valuable. Her house was as plain as could be. *As plain as Eleanor Bannister,* she heard her mother's sister say out of the past.

Eleanor looked around and saw that the past was here, in the girlish arrangement of embroidered pillows on the bed, in the dimity curtains her mother had made. She stared in dismay at Aunt Clara's dresser presiding in the corner, her childhood trinkets still marching across the length of a crocheted runner.

Chills ran over her. *This house*—she stood still, paralyzed by a sudden insight. *This house is the embodiment of my life.* She held on to the dresser. *I am sealed in here like a corpse in a tomb!*

Cleo glanced at her. "You feelin' shivery, Miz Bannister?"

"I'm fine," said Eleanor. *Fine—and as dead as if dirt were shoveled over me!*

Trembling, she moved across the room and reached into her closet. "Here, Cleo. Take these." She began pulling out the skirts and blouses she wore every day. Her church dresses. Her good black coat that she had wrapped herself in for so many winters she couldn't remember when she didn't have it.

"These is your good clothes!" Cleo said. "You don't aim to give these away, do you?"

"Will they sell?"

"Oh yes'm, they'll sell." Cleo pressed the black coat against her cheek. "You was wearing this the day the see-saw come down on me and broke my foot. You covered me with this coat till the doctor come."

A hundred years ago. I have to finish this before I faint! "Take everything!" she ordered. "Put it in my car. Call me when you're done, and I'll drive you home."

"Honk the horn!" said Cleo when they drove up with the car full of clothes. "Harley Rae's home by now. She'll come out and get 'em."

Eleanor peered at the unpainted house and the chickens pecking in the bare dirt around it. "She doesn't live with you, does she?"

"Just for now, till her and Dudley gets done with their courses. Saves us all a heap, being under one roof. Try honking again, Miz Bannister. She mighta dozed off."

"I see a child looking out."

"That's Lorena, the sick one. Reenie!" Cleo called. "We needs you out here!"

But it was Harley Rae who emerged, looking nothing like the waif Eleanor remembered. Trim, in a nice skirt. Her hair combed, her face made up.

"Why, Miss Bannister, hello!" She looked in at the loaded car. "Mama? My goodness! What do you have here?"

"A few things for your sale," Eleanor said.

"We wiped out everything!" said the jubilant Cleo. "Everything that wasn't from too long ago. Thems was nice things too," she amended hastily, "but they was hairlooms."

"If we could please get unloaded," Eleanor said.

"Of course, yes. You're wonderful, Miss Bannister, to bring all these things, and I'm sorry to impose on you further, but it would help so much if you could unload down at Evart's. We're using a storeroom there to mark everything, and Dudley can come out and have the car cleared in just a few minutes. I can call him right now and tell him you're on the way."

"Yes. Good." Harley Rae was pretty! Pretty and poised. How astonishing!

Opening the car door, Harley Rae said, "Get out now, Mama." But not unkindly. To Eleanor she said, "Thank you again. Thanks so much!"

"You're quite welcome. And good luck in your studies."

She might even write me a thank-you note, Eleanor mused as she drove away. By some miracle or other, Cleo's child had transformed herself, had risen out of that chicken house and become a lady. How on earth had she done it?

As she turned into her own driveway after Dudley had emptied the car, the answer to her wonderment presented itself: education had changed Harley Rae. That scruffy little girl in the tenth grade had listened to something, and some little bit of it had rubbed off. Something, thought Eleanor, that I might have said.

13

About four-thirty, Abel showed up at the kitchen door and looked through the glass at Eleanor, sitting at the table, her hands in her lap as if somebody had cast a spell over her.

He came in without knocking. "What is it?" he said.

She looked up blankly.

"Were you napping with your eyes open?"

"Sit down, Abel." The moment of euphoria she had experienced while reflecting on her possible influence on Harley Rae had passed swiftly when she looked again at her empty closet. "If you want a cup of coffee, the pot's on the stove."

"Honey-bun," he told her, "you know I don't drink coffee in the afternoon."

"I don't drink it at all, but I've had two cups. And don't call me honey-bun. It's a sticky, silly name inappropriate for a woman my age."

He took a chair quietly and sat looking at her as if he found her endlessly interesting. "I missed you today."

110

She had never popped in again while he was at work, but by mutual assent she continued to walk over to the cottage when he had finished for the day. It was a precious time they looked forward to. They strolled together through the cottage, Abel pointing out each new improvement and the two of them discussing what steps should be taken next to bring to completion the unspoken dream growing between them: to restore every room to its most perfect state.

"I decided you'd gone off with Grace and forgotten to mention you weren't coming by. But then I saw Grace passing and you not with her—"

"Abel," she interrupted, "I am in the midst of a revolution that from all indications is going to destroy me."

"Eleanor." He took her hand, her little paw, and gave it a squeeze. "What's the trouble, my dear?"

"It began the day you came, and now another frightful turmoil this morning has caused me to perform an unheralded act. A rash act without precedent."

He hid his alarm. "What was it, my dear?"

"I gave away my clothes."

"Oh, your *clothes!* Well, I know how that is. Turning loose of old favorites. It's like losing friends."

"Abel, I have given away *all* of my clothes. I have only what I'm wearing. And my nightgowns," she added. "And my underwear."

"Good thinking." He stared. "Hanging on to your underwear."

"This is not a joke!"

"I see that it isn't. It's an impressive gesture of generosity."

"It wasn't generosity," she answered sharply.

Abel sighed. "What was it, then?"

"Self-preservation, I thought at first." Eleanor bit her lip. "But now I believe it was reckless abandon."

"Reckless abandon?" Abel took time to clear his throat. "Who was the recipient?"

"Skinny Cleo Carter. Cleo Carter Block. A former student of mine."

"Oh. A woman."

"Well, certainly a woman! What man would come around asking for my clothes?"

He recovered quickly. "What I meant to say is she might be a woman I have met." He allowed himself a breath. "A smallish woman? With a cackling laugh, who cleaned the recreation room at the trailer park by the lake?"

"Yes, that's Cleo. She's been cleaning her whole life, and she does an excellent job." Eleanor stared at the breakfast dishes still on her counter, and the crumbs from the cinnamon rolls scattered on the table. "Cleo's daughter, Harley Rae, is having a sidewalk sale in front of Evart's."

"And that's where your clothes went, to Harley Rae's sale."

She resented the smile relaxing his face. "I'm told," she countered, "that Harley Rae's husband and Mr. Taylor have been engaged by you to work at the cottage."

"Dudley and Bill. Yes, I talked to them. Dudley is the young fellow who sold me my cap. He's Bill Taylor's son. I believe I told you that. Now I find out he's your friend's son-in-law. And the husband of Harley Rae, to whom you have given your clothes. Signposts everywhere," he said

happily. Then he noticed her annoyance. "But I didn't en-
gage the men. I just felt them out in case I need help with
one or two things." He added soothingly, "I wouldn't hire
anyone without discussing it first with the owner of the
house."

"Cleo said you plan to finish soon."

"By Christmas. Our goal," Abel reminded.

"Christmas, Abel, is months away."

"Eight weeks," he said cheerfully. "A sidewalk sale.
Why didn't I think of that?"

"On Saturday," said Eleanor, her gloom returning.
"Everything I own will be dancing in the wind for the
whole town to see. I have mortified myself, Abel."

"No, no." He patted her arm. "You're having second
thoughts, that's all."

He was reminding her that her previous second
thoughts had not amounted to much, but she was not
consoled. "I can't bear the idea of meeting women in the
street wearing my clothes."

Abel got to his feet. "Let's go now and get them back."

"I don't want them back! But I have to do something.
I've rendered myself naked!"

He brought her up gently to stand before him. "Miss
El, beloved, the stores are full of clothes."

"And banks are full of money, but it belongs to people
who don't throw it away!"

"You've always been careful with your money, Eleanor.
That's why you have it now to spend as you need it."

"I'm spending it right and left, as fast as I can! I'll turn
up poor, and then what will I do?"

"I'll look after you." He raised her chin and kissed her.

"You think I'm a feeble-minded woman, don't you? A lunatic."

"I think there's more to this than you've told me." He brought her against his chest.

"Yes, there is more," Eleanor said, her eyes shut. "It began with my mother's clothes. I've kept them all these years. I go sometimes and stand in the closet just to smell her fragrance again. Summer Roses. It's still there, Abel, in the handkerchiefs she left in all her pockets."

Eleanor brought her head up, listening suddenly to the clear *chack* of a bird beyond the window. "Do you hear that?"

"Your thrush?"

"No. It's a winter bird. A brown thrasher. He's here every fall, so sleek and sure of himself, kicking in the leaves. No other bird makes a sound like that." She gazed at Abel. "I wish I could make it." And then she was crying.

He calmed her with his large hands, stroking her back, his quiet breath in her ear. "It's all right, my love."

"My mother's dresses," she murmured, "were still as beautiful in my mind as they were the day she drove off with my father and didn't come back." Her ragged breath moved him, and he held her closer.

"Then this morning," she went on, "I saw them through Cleo's eyes. Outdated. Old. Ancient costumes no one would give a dime for."

She took the handkerchief Abel held out and asked through her tears, "Do men still carry handkerchiefs? Women don't. I see them in church, dragging out paper tissues when they have to sneeze."

Abel smiled. "My lady carries handkerchiefs. And she wears a wrapper." He kissed her again. "You didn't give away your wrapper, did you?"

She muffled her answer against his shoulder.

"It's time for supper," he said. "Let me cook tonight."

She brushed at her tears. "You're going to cook in my kitchen?"

"In the sardine can."

Eleanor smiled shakily. "Will there be room for me?"

"I can squeeze you in. If I throw out my socks and my ukulele."

14

A biting wind had come up while they talked in the kitchen. Eleanor, without the coat she no longer owned, huddled against Abel's side as they moved swiftly through the thicket to the backyard of the cottage, where his trailer was anchored, a bright blue apparition blooming in the dusk. It was a color Eleanor associated with hippies.

Abel insisted it was *sky* blue. That was why he had bought it, so that whatever weather he traveled through, he was always moving along with his own clear day. "What do you think of that?" he asked in response to her criticism.

"I think you made it up ten seconds ago." She was bemused, however, by the poetry in his answer and had adjusted to the garish appearance of the trailer against the restful green of her thicket.

More disturbing was the fact that Abel had not moved into the cottage according to his plan. His whole excuse at the beginning for wanting to work on the house had been so that he could get out of his cramped quarters. But as he kept putting off doing so, Eleanor's fears escalated. She

pictured a dawn departure, herself coming to her kitchen
window, looking out and seeing nothing. No truck, as
when he had been gone for two days. No trailer either. At
night she dreamed of Abel disappearing and awoke damp
with sweat. Whenever she was with him, she harped on
getting him settled in the house. Move today, she said. Or
Tuesday. Or next Friday at the latest.

"When the sign's right," Abel told her. It was refreshing,
he said, to do his work without the encumbrances of furniture, and shoes and overalls flung into the corners.
Eleanor clung to this reasoning and held fast to a hope that
he was envisioning the renovation, as she at times was, as a
finished piece of work that he was loath to mar with the
transfer of his belongings. A feeble hope at best, but it fos-
tered a measure of self-control and helped prevent her
from spoiling the peace they had regained in the kitchen.
Hurrying along beside Abel, she did wish they could take a
moment to peep in at the cottage, but Abel was already at
the trailer door, opening it, urging her in out of the cold.

On the one previous occasion of Eleanor's entering the
trailer, in a rage because of Abel's mysterious absence, she
had been aware, even through her anger, of the suffocat-
ing smallness of his surroundings. On this chilly evening
she welcomed the warmth and coziness, but in the glow of
the lamps his abode seemed even smaller than she remembered. A mere turtle's shell! A one-man operation
that she moved through timorously, fearful that her slightest misstep might dislodge something and bring four or
five other things tumbling down.

Abel, on the other hand, was perfectly at ease. "You be
the queen," he said, pointing out the only chair in what

served as living room and kitchen, and sleeping quarters too, if the couch she was appraising made down into a bed, which to all appearances it surely did.

"But I want to help," she protested.

"You can snap the beans." He brought a towel to spread over her only skirt and handed her a brown sack and a bowl to fill. Twirling an imaginary mustache, he announced that the chef would prepare Catalina Chicken. He grinned. "Straight off the label of a salad-dressing bottle."

She watched him stir together boiled chicken bits prepared earlier, whole cranberry sauce, dried onion-soup mix, and the bottled dressing that had supplied the recipe with its name. When he was done, he shoved the dish into the oven and put a small, scratched record on a turntable atop his TV.

"A little band I used to play in," he said to Eleanor; then he watched her face from the couch as the sounds of his trumpet solo filled the trailer. "Stardust" was the tune, a favorite of Eleanor's, and she said in a dreamy voice when it was over, "You never told me you were a musician."

"I played your father's violin, didn't I?"

"That was not a musical performance."

Abel laughed. "How would you know? You were asleep."

"What did you call your band?"

"The Dorsey Trotters, named for our drummer, Nick Dorsey, who wasn't kin to Tommy but claimed he was." Abel smiled. "We toured around for a few months, and then we all got jobs roofing houses."

She handed over the beans and went to the stove with him to watch as he stirred them with a bit of onion into a spoonful of olive oil that covered the bottom of an iron skillet. He whistled while he stirred, and after a few min-

utes he poured in a little water and left the covered skillet
to simmer.

"That isn't how I cook beans," Eleanor said.

"I like mine crispy but tender. Like you, Miss El."

Color heated her cheeks. "A trumpeter," she said, anxious to appear composed. "And now a cook. A roofer," she
added, "and a brazen carpenter who goes around forcing
himself on maiden ladies."

He led her to the sofa and drew her close.

Eleanor murmured, "What if I hadn't allowed myself to
ride in your truck?"

"What if you hadn't decided to come out in your nightgown and pick your figs?"

He kissed her, touched her, starting up in Eleanor's
mind a stampede of wild-eyed ponies, heads thrust forward, manes flying.

When they parted, she said in a trembling voice, "I
used to try to imagine what it would be like to kiss a man I
wasn't kin to."

"Was it anything like that?"

"I could never have imagined anything like that."
Whenever she thought of him, all sorts of things paraded
through her mind, embarrassing her, thrilling her, amaz-
ing her that desire sleeping so long could in old age lustily
awaken.

"During all this long, terrible day," she said, "I was able
to hang on only because I knew at the end of it there
would be you."

His hand moved again, caressing her throat, her breast,
the breast of an Eleanor she hadn't known existed, who
might at any minute take off her sweater, throw it on the
floor. Throw her skirt on the floor.

Abel stood. "I better see to the beans."

We should be married, Abel, her heart cried out.

Abel mistook her look. "You're starving, aren't you? If you were at home you'd be eating your Post Toasties." He took her hand and brought her to his table, a planklike affair he let down from the wall. He pulled up a stool. "Water," he said and put it before her. He brought out silverware, paper napkins, two large white plates. He took his chicken dish from the oven and served the bright green beans. He seated himself. "Shall I say the blessing?"

"I'd like to, if I may." Head bowed, she said, "Bless this food, dear God. And bless the hands that prepared it."

15

When they had finished the supper dishes, Eleanor washing, Abel drying and putting them away in the only places each would fit, he suggested they go over to the cottage. "I want to show you something."

"What? Tell me what it is." It was not their practice to visit the cottage at night. Abel liked to put work behind him when the working day was over, so it had to be something special he had planned to show her earlier. Something so important it couldn't wait until tomorrow. "Tell me, Abel!"

"You'll see." He brought her a jacket with two buttons missing, an old plaid mackinaw that held the smell of his skin. As he wrapped her in it, little celebrations like fireworks went off in her chest.

"You finished hanging the French doors, didn't you?"

"I did. And I'm halfway through with one of the bookcases you thought would look nice as a frame." He had discovered the paned French doors in the attic of the garage, where her father must have stored them when they had offered the house for rent. "But that's not what we're going to see."

"Close your eyes," he said when they arrived at the back steps of the cottage.

"This is silly!" Eleanor protested, but she felt the long-ago excitement of approaching a Christmas stocking.

"Now," Abel said. "Take a look."

He had led her into the kitchen and faced her toward the grand surprise, a gleaming porcelain sink installed in the drainboard.

She blinked, astonished. "How beautiful, Abel!" She clasped her hands in delight. "It's so white it's blinding! And it's the same style as the old one!" She grabbed his arm and hugged him. "Where on earth did you find it?"

"Look closer, my dear. It *is* the old one."

"What? It can't be." She bent to examine the spotless white bowl, reflecting the ceiling light. "The old sink was pitted. No good for anything!" She peered more closely. "In the old sink there were stains, Abel. Stains so deep nothing could get them out." She ran water from the faucet. "The old one leaked."

"This one won't leak." He kissed her cheek.

"The old sink," she marveled. "It's a miracle, Abel!"

"If you don't like it, I can take it out."

"Fine chance of that! This Cinderella story is back where it belongs." She cooed to it ecstatically, "Once you were a wreck, and now you're elegant!" She returned Abel's kiss. "I know you are capable of fixing almost any-thing, but I can't believe you fixed this."

"I wish I could say I did." He grinned ruefully. "But it's Bill Taylor who gets the credit. Refinishing porcelain is what he did in Houston. He took me to his old shop there and let me watch him."

"That's where you were?" Eleanor stared, stricken. "Preparing this lovely surprise for me?" Tears sprang to her eyes. "And then you came home to a screaming virago."

"I'm not sure what that is, but I'm sure you're not it."

"I was afraid, Abel."

He tucked an arm around her waist. "Afraid I wasn't coming back?"

She buried her face against his chest. "Someday you may not."

"And someday we may be millionaires," he answered lightly. "Let's forget worry for now, okay? Let's enjoy the rejuvenation of the honeymoon cottage."

"It does look almost the way I dreamed it."

"Wait till it gets its finishing touches." His satisfied gaze swept the kitchen. "I like the way the cabinets turned out, and now that the sink is in—"

"Enthroned," corrected Eleanor, admiring the wooden drainboard Abel had spent hours smoothing and staining.

"That polyurethane does a good job," he said. "It won't let water in like varnish does when the new wears off."

Eleanor sighed. "If you had listened to my scoldings, you would have thrown the sink to the junk man. But you stood your ground, knowing how right it would be, how it would pull everything together and the kitchen would become again the one my mother enjoyed as a bride."

Together they gazed at the old wainscoting Abel had sanded and painted. Eleanor, with his assistance, had papered above it with a flower-sprigged pattern Grace had helped her choose. Then Grace had made curtains for the windows. The big X's, Abel called them, because of the style Grace insisted was in keeping with the period: thin cotton panels slipped onto rods at the top and bottom of each window and then gathered midway with flower-embroidered ties to match the paper. Plain gray linoleum covered the floor.

Eleanor said happily, "A modern sink would have ruined everything."

"Besides costing you a bundle," Abel said. "Bill was so glad for a chance to get his hand back in, he hardly charged anything, and you should have seen those fellows he used to work with, all standing around watching, as happy as if they were having birthdays."

"We could cook in here tomorrow. Or," Eleanor added hastily, "someone could. It's all done, isn't it?"

"Done in here, and the rest is coming along, but there's still work to do." He led the way to the tiny living room, where he had built a window seat across the east wall and incorporated a gas heater into a recessed area that had once held a chimney. The French doors were folded elegantly against the inner walls of the dining room entry. The kitchen shone beyond, and across the hall were the two bedrooms, white and federal blue, with the bathroom between.

"I need to touch up this paint." Abel pointed out places he had nicked while installing the doors. "And I've put off doing the hammered-tin ceilings in the bedrooms until the Taylors can help me give them a good cleaning."

"You've loved doing this, haven't you?" Eleanor wrapped her arms around him. "I'm so proud of you, Abel."

He lifted her chin with gentle fingers. "It was a dandy house to start with. You were wise to decide not to let it rot down."

She looked pensively at the worn face she loved so much she had to restrain herself from constantly caressing it. "You calmly go about your business while I pop and crackle like an old stove, shooting out sparks before I even know the story."

"Old stoves are the best," he said. "Like old sinks." He bent to kiss her. "We'd better go. It's cold in here."

Walking back toward the house under a thin rind of moon, Abel said, "If it's all right with you, I'll have a talk with Dudley and Bill and see when they can come."

"I'm sure Dudley will be glad for the extra money. He's enrolled in electronics school, and Harley Rae's doing everything under the sun to get herself through college."

"He's never mentioned children."

"They have one daughter. Nine or ten, I'd say."

"About the same age as Abby."

Eleanor said quietly, "What does Abby look like?" He had never shown her a picture, never talked much about her, but when he did mention her it was obvious how much he loved her.

"Oh," he said in his usual offhanded way, "I suppose she looks pretty much like any ten-year-old, getting gangly, a little grubby sometimes. As pouty and sunny as the weather." He squeezed Eleanor's hand. "You're shivering, Miss El. Let's pep it up."

They walked on, Eleanor still curious. "You're a grandfather. And you have a son-in-law. I know so little about your other life." How much did it matter that he kept it to himself? How much did he worry without ever speaking of it?

Not speaking of it now, he changed the subject. "What are your plans for tomorrow?" he said. "Are you going clothes shopping?"

"I have to, don't I, after this morning's performance." Her interlude with Cleo seemed like a dream now. Or more aptly, a nightmare. "If I don't buy a few things, I'll have to keep on wearing this same old skirt until somebody says something."

"Grace." Abel laughed.

"I'm going to take her with me. If she's not in on everything at the start, she's hurt when she finds out. But I hate to admit to her that I've become a woman with nothing in her closet but a row of shoes! Grace thinks I'm practical. She depends on me."

"I think you've turned a corner in your life, entered a new phase." Abel lifted a yaupon branch so she could pass safely under it. "Giving away your clothes was a good idea."

"You're trying to make me feel less irresponsible."

"You should be pleased with yourself. Not everyone at our time of life has the courage to kick over the traces the way you've done." His voice resonated wistfully. "It puts a new slant on everything."

Eleanor teased, "We'll see what kind of slant it is when I get my bank statement."

A cold wind sent a shower of leaves skittering across their path.

"Do you have any serious regrets, Miss El, about the money you've spent on the house?"

"Sometimes I feel a miserly twinge." She opened her back door and Abel followed her into the kitchen, where she stopped to gaze around. "Then I look at this place, drab as a brown mule, and I wonder how I've stood its ugliness all these years."

"I'm fond of this room." Abel pulled out a chair for her. "It's where I first tasted your fig preserves."

She sat down, brushing cinnamon-roll crumbs into her hand and then into a saucer. "This morning when Cleo was here, Abel, I lost my place."

He frowned. "What do you mean 'your place'?"

"I lost it the way a person does when he's reading and something interrupts him. He looks up, and when he looks back, he can't find where he was."

"What were you reading?"

"Nothing, Abel! I was having my tea. It was a bird-singy morning, Cleo said. Then it all went wrong."

"Ah, I see. The revolution flared up."

"Revolution," she said wryly. "How melodramatic that sounds now." She touched his hand. "So out of keeping with the nice meal you fixed, and your wonderful surprise, and the lovely way the house is turning out." She sighed. "But a revolution is what it feels like still. Like warring forces battling inside me."

He gazed at her troubled face. "I'd like to understand this."

"So would I." She picked up a missed crumb and absently laid it on her tongue. "When I brought out Mother's clothes and Cleo said no one would want them, it was like lightning had struck me. Everything lost its familiarity. It seemed like a time-warp thing, like Alice in Wonderland."

"Never read it," he said, "but maybe I get the picture."

She answered in a rush of despair, "It was so physically upsetting it made me dizzy. I got Cleo out of that closet and on to my bedroom while I could still think, but there were all those dead ancestors in the hall that she kept chattering about, and then when we got there, she said, *This is where you sleep!* as if my bed were some kind of Civil War memorial! As if I were a relic, a piece of my mother's clothes."

"Miss El, honey—"

Her voice rose. "I *hated* having my room on view! You don't know what an awful feeling it gave me to see Cleo looking so pleased at my things. At my *self* on exhibit! Cleo standing there wasn't seeing a bed and a dresser, she was seeing her old teacher, Eleanor Bannister, as she really is: prim, aging, so much a part of her surroundings even I couldn't distinguish where I began or ended."

She shook her head. "This house and everything in it is what I am! It's *all* I am after seventy years!"

"That's not true, Eleanor."

"It *is* true. The truth was right there in front of me: Cleo—an old woman herself!—holding up my black coat, telling me it was the coat I wore when she was in the fifth grade! A lifetime ago, Abel, and I still owned it. I was still wearing it!"

"Cleo could have been mistaken."

"She was not mistaken! She could have said something similar about almost everything I brought out of that closet. All the things I've held on to to make time stand still—or to make it go backward!" Eleanor shuddered. "Well, I got rid of it! I threw it all out, every last thing."

"Good for you," Abel said. "Now you'll feel better."

"Now I feel worse! Stripped naked."

He regarded her thoughtfully. "In the middle of the cross fire."

"That's it exactly! I threw away the old and there isn't any new."

"Miss El." He spoke carefully. "I expect the new has been hanging around backstage for quite a while. The new," he said softly, "is what made you bust loose and toss away your treasures."

She frowned darkly. "I don't see that at all!"

Abel waited a moment and then went on. "You said this afternoon the turmoil started with me, when I showed up. I think it was simmering pretty good before I got here."

"If you're going to talk about signposts—!"

"Not right now." His gaze rested gently on her anguished face. "I'm going to talk about stirrings that can start up inside a person. Like redbugs crawling under your skin, producing an itch that there's no way to scratch."

Eleanor said bitterly, "You're perilously close to standing in a pulpit, about to preach on a subject you don't understand yourself."

"Oh, I understand it," he answered steadily. "You rock along for a while, years maybe, feeling pretty good about everything, feeling pretty pleased with yourself about how well you're doing, and then the redbugs pile in. Dissatisfactions. Restlessness you can't get to the heart of. Things start looking gray that used to look like sunrises. Are you with me, Miss El?"

She lowered her eyes, her mouth a tight bundle.

Abel placed a hand over hers. "When you're obsessed that way, the feeling grows in you that you've got to make a move, you've got to change things or you'll jump out of your skin. You don't know if you're lonely or if what you need is to get as far away from everybody as you possibly can."

"You're describing yourself!" she lashed out suddenly. "You're talking about a drifter."

"Maybe I am." He paused, blinking. "I expect I am. But I'm talking more about feeling the *urge* to drift and not being able to respond to it because you're too rooted in your life to pick up and move along."

"I have never in my life wanted to live anywhere except here!"

"But haven't you at times wanted to live differently? To find another way?"

To kick up my heels and dance? "No!" she said.

He leaned away from her and got out of his chair and stood over her. "Then I was mistaken. It was my feeling when I met you that here's a beautiful woman, as ripe as these figs, ready to be picked."

Eleanor gasped. "You played on my emotions! For your own gratification!"

"I played your violin," he said in a voice so low she could hardly hear him. "I ate at your table. I fell in love with you."

"You did not fall in love! Love isn't static. It doesn't stand in one place and not turn into anything."

"Like marriage?" he said. "I've wanted to marry you ever since that night in the thicket when your thrush sang." Eleanor could see the throbbing at the base of his throat. "I want to live in the cottage with you and be all you want me to be, but I don't know if I've whipped those redbugs. I don't know if I've stripped naked as you did today, or if I'm only fooling myself and one morning I'll wake up and go back on the road again." He looked sadly at her. "What kind of husband would a man like that make?"

She heard him go out. She sat there in his mackinaw that was missing two buttons, then hurried to the window to watch his shadowy figure cross the lawn and pass through the thicket. A square of light jumped out of the darkness as the trailer door opened; then it vanished, closing on his turtle shell, closing on Abel Brown's compact life, where there was room only for him and his uncertainties.

Eleanor lay, dry-eyed, watching car lights turning onto Tennessee, flashing around her bedroom walls. She said aloud, "He loves me; he wants to marry me."

The answer came back: *If he did, he would.*

She got up at two for a drink of water. From where she stood in her dark kitchen, she could see that his light was on. *He can't sleep either,* she thought with satisfaction. *In the morning he'll come knocking on my door.*

Then she caught her breath. *He was coming now!* Reversing his earlier path through the thicket, his dark form strode purposefully toward her. She put her hands to her breast. Did he plan to pound on the door? Wake her up, get down on his knees? Her heart beat wildly.

I should put on a robe.

There's no time for a robe!

She waited, rooted, thinking of what she might say, how she might take back the words she had flung at him.

Waited.

For nothing.

At the window again, she saw him going away from her. Saw his light go out. Heard his truck start up.

She let a few minutes go by, and more minutes, thinking, *He'll come back.* Thinking, *Where has he gone?* Praying pitiful little whimpering prayers she was ashamed of. Filling with anger that drained away quickly and left her crying.

Stiff and aching, she went back to her bed and turned on the light. Her daybook lay on the table where she had left it after she came home from dropping off her clothes at Evart's. She read the last entry:

> *Today I was funneled into a hopper and came out raw and bare. What will I put on myself that will be any different from what covered me before?*

What indeed?

She lay down again, staring at a rain stain on the ceiling, a cherub's face, its lips pursed, puffing out breezes. Zephyrs, she had called them in her poetic youth.

And now she was old.

She sat up and wrote again in her book:

> *Is there any time left for me to become more than a displaced person, my past spent, my future nonexistent? Or have I used it all up, sniveling and nattering, pinching the minutes and letting the precious years run out the door?*

She went to sleep finally, unaware that for the first time her daybook entry was not addressed to her mother and father.

16

Eleanor woke up late with the bedside light still burning. She sat up in a panic. Nine-thirty! Grace would be calling, wanting to know why she hadn't honked for her, why she hadn't picked up her paper.

The telephone rang. "You haven't picked up your paper. Are you sick, Eleanor?"

"No, I am not sick! I overslept. I'll be along in a minute."

"I'll be out on the porch."

"It's too cold to stand outside! Wait in your living room. You can see me through the window."

"I'll be on *your* porch."

"For heaven's sake! We're not going to a fire."

"Toodle-loo," said Grace, plunking down the phone.

Eleanor flung on her only outfit and skipped her morning tea. As she went out the front door to pick up her paper, she saw that Grace had beaten her to it and, from the rumpled look of it, had already read the first section.

"I'll get the car," Eleanor told her. "Stay right here." Hurrying down the driveway, she tried unsuccessfully to spot Abel's truck through the thicket.

Off having breakfast, she prayed silently.

She sat in the cold car for a minute, composing herself. *It will be all right.* She straightened her hair in the rearview mirror. She would get the clothes she needed, buy Grace a nice lunch, and when she got home Abel would be home too. She would go straight over there and tell him to stop talking nonsense; they were going to get married no matter what his objections were. *Redbugs!* Imagine.

Grace knocked on the window. "What's the matter now? Can't you get the car started?"

"Get in!" barked Eleanor. "And shut the door firmly."

Grace looked up from digging in her purse for her sunglasses and saw that Eleanor had driven onto the open highway, leaving Grover behind.

"I thought we were going shopping."

"We are."

"Where?"

"Down the road somewhere."

"We're going to wander aimlessly?" Grace sat back. "How refreshing."

"I'm tired of Polly's 'beautiful clothes at beautiful prices.' She charges an arm and a leg even for a petticoat. Let's look around Claremont."

"Claremont!" said Grace. "We're going all the way over there and you didn't tell me? I could have brought my list." Grace had given up highway driving when her husband died. "I need four or five things I can't find at home, but without my list, I can't think of a one of them."

"Maybe if you sit quietly, you'll remember."

Instead Grace burst out, "I know what you're doing! You're sneaking out of town to buy a TV!"

"I have a TV, Grace. Why would I want another one?"

"Yours doesn't work."

"Of course it works."

"Remember the last Rose Parade? Those lovely floats and all of them green?"

"My TV is for watching the news. It doesn't matter if the news is green."

"If you buy a TV out of town, Eleanor, Porter's won't come fix it when it goes on the blink. You'll have to call the store where you bought it, and they'll stick it to you, a service fee and mileage to boot. How many miles is it?"

"Thirty-five."

"Fifteen cents every time a number changes. Oh!" she said suddenly. "Earl Grey tea! That was on my list. Yes. At the top. Isn't the human mind a remarkable thing?"

Coming into Claremont, Eleanor said, "What is the name of that discount place where they sell ladies' clothing?"

"Lorimor's? Are we going *there*?"

"I thought we might."

"I've never been there!"

"Neither have I."

"Sissy has," Grace said breathlessly. "The women all undress in the same big dressing room. They have full-length mirrors on every wall so everybody sees everybody else in their underwear, front and back."

"You don't have to try on anything if you feel intimidated."

"Obviously you don't know what kind of underwear young girls are wearing. Sissy says their breasts bulge out of their skimpy brassieres and their underpants are practically G-strings."

"Maybe we'll learn something."

"Not anything we need to know. At least nothing I need to know." A new thought struck her. "Eleanor! Are you going to buy your trousseau?"

"No, Grace."

"You'd tell me, wouldn't you? I'm your best friend. Well, a close friend anyway."

"I am not buying wedding clothes," Eleanor said. "But I do need to tell you something." As simply as she could, she explained. "When I opened my closet door to look for something for Harley Rae's sale, I decided all at once to give Cleo everything."

"Everything?"

"All my clothes. Except what I'm wearing and my personal lingerie."

"You mean your dresses? And your black coat? Why, Eleanor, you've had that black coat—"

"I know how long I've had it! I've gotten my money's worth, wouldn't you say?"

Grace couldn't say anything. When Eleanor stopped the car, she turned and looked at her.

"What is it, Grace?"

"I never heard of anyone giving away all their clothes."

"Abel thought it was a good idea." Eleanor kept her grip on the steering wheel. "Now, for your part: Tomorrow morning will you go down to the sale—early, Grace—and buy my wrapper?"

"Your paisley wrapper?"

"Yes."

"Why?"

"Because as one of my dearest friends I'm asking you to. Pay whatever is marked on it, and I'll pay you back. And you don't need to mention who it's for."

Eleanor and Grace were stunned by the dressing room (bigger than the fellowship hall at the Presbyterian Church) and by the youthful pulchritude throbbing around them.

"How do they get those figures?" Grace whispered. "In my very best days I never looked like that."

"Stand behind me," Eleanor instructed. "I want to be covered in at least one direction."

Taken as a whole, it was an interesting excursion. The building didn't catch fire while they had their clothes off, as Grace anticipated. A woman undressing next to her from Prater Creek didn't know her Cousin Mildred, as Grace was sure she would, it being such a small place and Mildred having lived there forever. Her parents too. But it was exciting just the same, for both Grace and Eleanor, to be among a crowd of women baring their bodies. To be a *part* of such a crowd! And to finally lose their self-consciousness in the comforting realization that except for the young girls, they looked about as good as anyone else.

"Better than some," Grace declared as they drove home. "Did you see that woman who'd had her breasts raised? Twice, it looked like—and she didn't mind talking about it."

"Were the surgeries successful?"

"At the time, I guess they were. But if she doesn't die first she'll need to do it again." Grace sighed. "If I were going to have plastic surgery, I'd like my chin lifted. My dewlap, you know. I'd have that cut out and the flap stitched up." She smoothed the drooping skin beneath her chin. "I believe it might make a world of difference."

Eleanor only half listened. She had decided while they were having lunch that Abel, lying awake last night, had thought of something he needed for the cottage and that was where he had gone. Probably into Houston, leaving early to be there when the doors opened so he could get back in time for a full day's work. Absent-mindedly, he had walked over to tell her and then realized the time and turned around and gone back.

Also, the excitement of shopping had taken the edge off the scene in her kitchen. It seemed as she drove along with Grace's chatter in the background that it was not the earth-shaking event she had thought at first but more the kind of conversation in which a person reveals something he puzzles about at times. A thing he wants to air and then put away again in its place in his brain, a place something like a cupboard where he keeps old scrapbooks and photographs and letters. She herself had such a cupboard, located, as she pictured it, above her right ear.

Her spirits lifted, and she began thinking of her purchases: two new church dresses for warmer weather and two to carry her through the winter, a nice black suit for funerals, and a white silky blouse to dress it up for other occasions. She had two new skirts, two sweaters, a new coat (tan this time), two other blouses—or shirts, really—that she could wear to the library and the grocery store, and finally her favorite thing of all: a pair of pants. Tweed. Straight-legged and neatly fitted over her rear. Grace had convinced her that she needed a sporty kind of contrasting jacket, and she had bought that too.

"How much did you spend?" Grace asked, ascertaining from Eleanor's expression that she was thinking of her clothes.

"I didn't add it up."

"You wrote a check."

"I don't recall exactly how much it was."

"A thousand dollars?"

"I'm not made of money!"

Grace turned a wise look out the window. "Well, I'm not so sure you're not. All the remodeling you're doing and the flouncing around with your gentleman friend." She turned back to Eleanor. "I had a thrilling day. I felt rich myself, and free in a way, though I don't know what from." A contented smile crossed her face. "If you decide to get married, Eleanor, could I give you a shower?"

At home again, Eleanor dropped Grace off, waiting as patiently as she could for Grace to get her purchases from the back seat, and then she drove around the block, intending to go straight to Abel, but when she turned in at the cottage, the truck wasn't there.

"Gone to town for something," she assured herself. But it was late for that. Most of the stores were closed.

Eating, she thought. She drove through town to no avail; then with a sudden rush of joy she realized where he must be. On Tennessee Street. At her house! She hadn't seen him when she let Grace out because he hadn't yet arrived. He was going around the block one way while she went the other.

But the truck was not in her driveway either. She drove mindlessly into the garage and saw as she came out a white envelope attached to her screened porch door with a strip of duct tape. She made herself carry it inside and lay it on the table while she took her packages into her bedroom.

Heart aflutter, she reminded herself that the trailer was still there. Abel was not really gone or he would have taken the trailer. *Unless.* She had to sit suddenly on the bed. Unless he was off somewhere locating a trailer park. A new place to live. Saving himself the trouble of dragging the trailer up and down highways before he was certain where he was headed.

She put off looking at the note. She combed her hair and went to the bathroom. She looked pale, she saw in the lavatory mirror. Sick. Old. Finally, resolutely, she went into the kitchen and opened the envelope.

It contained one sheet of paper and two sentences in a handwriting she realized she was seeing for the first time. How little she knew of this man on whom her whole life depended!

She scanned what he had written and then returned to the start and read it aloud: "Something came up. I'll be gone a few days. Love, A."

He had written *Love*. The kitchen came into focus. His writing was strong, masculine. *Dependable*. He would be back. He *would* be back!

She ate something (she couldn't think afterward what it was), and then she sat down in the living room with the note, scrutinizing its words under the lamp.

Few. A *few* days. He could have said several days. That would be more like two, or three at the most. How many was a few days? Four? Five? She would not start looking for him before Tuesday. Or Monday night. Wednesday was the latest he would turn into her driveway and tell her what had come up.

What could possibly have come up?

17

"A *few* days!" Eleanor grumbled on Monday evening. "More like a week!" It felt like a month. She had worked herself into a tizzy over the weekend, unable to keep from going back and forth to the kitchen window, expecting any moment to witness Abel's return and growing more fearful each time she saw only her blank driveway and no sign of the truck.

Something could have happened to him. In her mind she went through a wreck from start to finish, even as far as the hospital, where she saw Abel lying with both legs broken but still faintly breathing. She pictured him wandering up to Canada, scratching his redbugs. On a roof somewhere in Oklahoma. Building fences in Nebraska.

When she couldn't stand it a minute longer, she telephoned Grace. "Tomorrow," she said with assumed carelessness, "I am going to San Antonio."

"San Antonio!"

"It's only a hundred miles farther than Claremont. We can spend the night at the Menger and tour the Alamo."

"You're including me?"

"I can't go alone. In an unfamiliar city, who would read the street signs while I'm watching the traffic?"

"What a flattering invitation, Eleanor. Do you think Abel is in San Antonio? Is that why you're going?"

"I'm going because I need a vacation!"

"As long as I've known you, you've never taken a vacation. Remember that time I wanted you to go on the bus with me to Dallas to see my sister, and you wouldn't go even though you had three months off and nothing to do?"

"I was younger then."

"All the more reason you won't go now. You're really mad at Abel, aren't you?"

"I am provoked, Grace. He is at the point of completing the renovation, and he drives merrily away with no thought of his responsibilities and leaves only a scrap of paper to let me know he has gone."

"Stole away in the night. Like a thief." Grace giggled.

Eleanor hung up.

Grace called back. "I was joking, Eleanor. Abel Brown is a nice man. I personally consider him very responsible. Some men with as much to do as he has wouldn't have taken the time to paint my windowsills and repair my sidewalk. I'm sure he had a good reason for leaving and will be back the first chance he gets."

"I'll tell him of your endorsement. If I ever speak to him again."

Early Tuesday morning Eleanor was contemplating her travel plans while pouring milk on her cereal at the kitchen sink. Glancing by habit toward the thicket, she saw a child wandering in it. A stranger, a small girl.

Sitting down on my bench!

She grabbed her paisley wrapper, which Grace had rescued at the sale, and rushed out to set the intruder straight.

"This is private property!" she said, out of breath when she got there. "What are you doing here?"

"Shh!" The child pointed upward. "I'm talking to that squirrel." She grinned at Eleanor. "He's about as fussy as you are."

"Who are your parents?" Eleanor demanded.

The smile vanished. "Nobody you'd know." The child stuck out her chin. "I'm not hurting anything. Why can't I sit here?"

"Because you were not invited to sit here."

"I was too! My Grampa invited me. His friend owns this place."

"What?"

"It's better manners to say, 'Pardon me?' when you don't understand something."

Eleanor sank down beside her. "Is your name Abby?"

"No, it isn't. It's Abigail Louise, but my Grampa calls me Abby."

Eleanor's thoughts did cartwheels. "Why aren't you in school?"

"Because my school is in Marshall and I'm here."

"How long will you be here?"

"Till my mother finds my father."

"*Finds* him?"

"He went off a while back." The child began picking heart-shaped leaves off a climbing vine. "He's done that before. But this time my mom's sick of it. He's either coming back to stay or she's going to divorce him."

Eleanor pressed fingertips to her brow. "Where is your grandfather?"

"He's trying to fix breakfast, but we forgot to get milk and the bread molded, so we aren't having much."

"Where did you sleep last night?"

"On the couch in the trailer. It makes down."

"And your grandfather?"

"In the truck."

"I don't see the truck."

Abby turned and pointed. "It's parked on the other side, up against the windows so I wouldn't be scared in there by myself. When I stayed with Grampa before, me and my mom, he put a camper on his truck. He may get another one."

"If you're here that long."

"Oh, I'll be here. My Grampa says this is a big country to find one man in."

Eleanor closed her eyes. "Please go and tell your grand-father I am preparing breakfast at my house for the two of you."

"Who will I tell him you are?"

"Miss Eleanor Bannister."

"The famous Miss El?" The impish grin returned. "I know all about you."

"I'm sure you do not!"

"I know it's your house Grampa is working on. And you live"—she whirled around—"right over there, I bet."

Eleanor got to her feet and started off at a rapid pace. "I shall expect you shortly."

Abigail called after her, "Do you have a cat?"

"No, I do not."

"Or a dog?"

"No!"

In her house again, Eleanor took time to make a quick call. "San Antonio is off," she said into the phone.

"Abel—?"

"Back. And he has someone with him."

"Who?" Grace gasped. "He didn't go off and get married, did he?"

"His granddaughter, Grace."

"Granddaughter!"

"Nine years old."

"Shouldn't she be in school?"

"Exactly," said Eleanor.

"I've seen the Alamo, so never mind that, but if he has a granddaughter, he must have had a wife. Did you know he had a wife?"

"He did mention a wife once."

"You didn't mention it to me. Oh, I can see them! They're coming out of the thicket. She's small for her age. Are they coming for breakfast?"

"I have to go, Grace."

"Well, are they, Eleanor?"

"I'm hanging up now, and you should do the same."

Eleanor had never spent such an exhausting morning. Over cereal and toast she saw how haggard Abel looked, though he kept smiling at her, which made her long to put her arms around him. However, demonstrations of affection were out of the question. With Abigail at the table, all meaningful conversation was out of the question too.

"You may go and watch TV," Eleanor said, clearing the dishes.

Abigail wandered off, but she was heard coming back before Eleanor had learned much more than that Kit had telephoned to tell Abel her plans, and after much discussion he had extracted a promise that she would not take the child with her.

"What did she say when you got there?"

"She'd already left. Left her daughter sitting on a suitcase, and a note telling me where to put the key."

Abigail reentered the kitchen. "Everything's green on that TV."

"Maybe you can adjust it."

"I'll see if I can." Abel went out, and above the clinking of the dishes Eleanor heard the two of them talking companionably in the living room.

The rest of the morning crept by in a similar fashion: a swift exchange of information while Abby was in the bathroom; another few words when Eleanor sent her out for the paper.

Abel tried several times to put an end to the visit. "This is wearing you out," he told Eleanor, but she wouldn't let him go.

"I have to know, Abel, how you're going to handle this!"

"How can I tell you when I don't know myself?"

At last at the lunch table, Abby began nodding. Joy surged in Eleanor, followed by a guilty stab of pity for the uprooted child, who was sure to be aware of the disruption her presence was causing.

"You need a nap," announced Eleanor. "Go and lie down in the spare bedroom, Abby."

"No," Abel said. "I'm taking her to the trailer."

"She'll be perfectly fine here."

"No, Eleanor."

"Yes, Abel!"

Abby slid from her chair. "I'm going to lie on the porch glider and look at the birds."

She was asleep in two minutes.

"It was a long ride," Abel said. "Before that there was a lot to do, gathering up Abby's things and closing Kit's house. She said she'd paid her rent in advance, but she was two months behind. I made up the difference and bribed the landlord not to cut off the utilities. I said she'd be back, but God knows if she will."

Eleanor led him, still talking, into the living room and shut the door. "We have to make arrangements." She settled him on the couch.

He lay back with his eyes closed. "What kind of arrangements?"

"About Abigail, of course!" *Poor weary man.* Less stridently she said, "You were right, Abel, not to allow Kit to drag Abigail around the country in pursuit of that man—"

"Dad, he's called," Abel rebuked gently. "Don Florentino. He's not a bad fellow. Just unpredictable. Undependable." He blinked sleepily at Eleanor. "Something like me, as you once remarked."

"Ants in his pants."

"Redbugs too."

Eleanor held back tears and the desire to wrap her arms around him. "The redbug question will have to wait for now. We have to decide how to proceed with this child."

He sat forward. "Miss El, honey. That's not your worry. It's my responsibility, and I'll take care of it."

"How, Abel?"

"First I'll get milk and bread." He smiled tiredly. "Then in the morning we'll go from there. She won't be under *your* feet. I promise you that."

"No, she'll be under yours. If you can't work when I'm in the cottage, Abel, how will you handle a child asking questions all the time, whining after a while? She'll get out of sorts, you know. She'll want to be entertained."

"She can play in the yard."

"When it's rainy and cold?"

"God, Eleanor." He rubbed his eyes. "I'll work it out as the problems come up."

"Nine or ten will come up before lunchtime. And then there'll be the afternoons. And the evenings after that. Abigail needs to be in school."

Abel blinked. "I forgot about school."

"I've thought about it all morning. I've thought everything out. Later this afternoon we'll move her things over here, and then in the morning—"

"Wait. Wait a minute."

"It's perfectly plain she needs to live with me."

Abel got to his feet. "I am not unloading a child on you."

"Indeed you aren't. If you tried to, I wouldn't let you. Sit down, Abel. This is my idea, and I want you to listen to it. The most basic thing is that you don't have room for her. You hardly have room enough for yourself."

"We can sleep in the cottage."

"No, you cannot. I won't allow it."

"Eleanor! You spent a whole month trying to get me to move in there! Now you won't let me."

"You missed your chance. Now, listen, please. She will have her own room here. A young girl needs privacy."

"So does an old girl. And you won't have any!"

"Let me tell you something, Abel Brown. I have not given birth, but I have spent most of my life dealing with children. They have coughed in my face, vomited in my lap, and put living crawfish in my coat pockets, but they have never been rude to me more than once. Furthermore, some of them have even loved me."

"I'm sure of that."

"Abel, I know how to care for children, and I want to care for this one."

"I appreciate your kindness. More than you'll ever know, my dear. But I can't let you. This is not the time of your life to be taking on a child day and night. I won't have that. Abby and I will get along. It'll take a little doing, but eventually we'll hit our stride."

"You're half dead now! By tomorrow night you'll be in a coma."

"How will you be if you have her over here?"

"I will set up a routine and we will manage famously. You have to approach this from a practical point of view. Furthermore, there is not enough oxygen in that trailer to support two lives!"

He smiled faintly. "That's quite an argument, Miss El. But the answer is no."

"Please!"

"It's not right."

"It *is* right. When Abby wakes up, we'll explain everything to her. Her manners need sharpening, but she's a nice child, a spirited child. I admire that. She will understand this is best for everyone."

"There's no telling how long she'll be here."

"We'll manage it, Abel."

He shook his head and gave up. "All right. We'll try it a few days, but as soon as you've had enough, she's coming back to me."

"Agreed," said Eleanor.

They looked at each other. Long, starved looks that made them both tremble.

"The bottom dropped out on us," Abel murmured. "I haven't even found out how the shopping trip went."

"Abel," she said, "if you go away again and don't tell me where, it will probably kill me."

He took her face between his hands and kissed her mouth, her closed eyelids. "Every minute I was gone, I was trying to get back here."

18

"This room will be yours," Eleanor said, standing in the late-evening sun filtering into her parents' bedroom through curtains that had always hung there. *Marvelous old lace,* Eleanor thought, wondering how it would hold up in proximity to an active child.

Abigail stood in the doorway, silent as a photograph. After the child's nap, Eleanor had explained how they had worked things out for everyone's comfort. Without comment, Abigail had gone off with Abel and after a while returned alone with a bulging duffel bag and a few items of clothing dangling from hangers.

Eleanor, eyeing one of them, tried to imagine the child actually wearing that long, draggy shirt with hearts all over it. And if so, *where*?

"I sleep in it," said Abby, reading her stare. "I guess you wear those peachy-colored buttoned-up nightgowns my Granny Irene always wore."

Abel's former wife. Eleanor's hackles rose. "Sometimes," she said crisply, "I don't wear anything." An outright lie (except for that one sleepless night), but it had its effect.

"Nothing?" exclaimed Abby. "You're making that up!"

"Why do you think so? Don't I look like a lady who might sleep in the nude?"

"In the nude!" Abby hooted. "Do you mean buck naked?"

"We have work to do here!" Eleanor said sharply. "Hang your things in the closet, Abigail. Tomorrow I'll empty the dresser drawers and you'll have a place for your other belongings." She glanced toward the hall. "You know where the bathroom is. The light switch, remember, is right by the door."

"Are we going to bed now? The sun is still shining."

Eleanor wished for a cataclysmic event that would bring down night at once, but she asked gallantly, "What would you like to do before you go to sleep?"

"Write my mother a letter. I can't mail it yet since I don't know where she is. But I'll have it ready when I do know."

"An excellent plan. I'll get some paper, and then we'll take a few minutes to talk about school."

When Eleanor returned with a sheet of white stationery and an envelope, Abigail was holding one of Mrs. Bannister's dresses pressed to her nose. "Whose is this?"

"My mother's," said Eleanor.

"It smells like roses."

"Summer Roses." Eleanor's harried look softened. "That was the fragrance my mother wore."

"Perfume, you mean?"

"Ladies in that day perfumed themselves with fragrance. Or scent, some called it."

"Fragrance is nicer. Scent is like skunks. Do you have skunks around here?"

"None that I know of."

"We had skunks in Marshall. One under our house. A couple of times I saw him go under there. Or it might have been a she."

Eleanor held out the writing paper. "You may compose your letter at the desk over there."

"I'd rather lie on the floor."

"As you please," said Eleanor, so weary she could faint, and there was the phone ringing!

"I'll get it!" said Abigail, hopping up.

"Ask who is calling. If it's Miss Grace tell her I'll call her tomorrow."

Abigail came back. "It's a lady named Harley Rae. She said if you're busy she could call you later. I think it's about me."

Harley Rae had heard from her father-in-law that Mr. Brown had spoken to the principal at the school and made arrangements for his granddaughter to enroll. If Miss Bannister liked, Reenie could walk over in the morning and the girls could go together. "Unless, of course, you'd rather take her yourself."

"Not at all," said Eleanor, so grateful she could cry. "I'll have Abigail ready."

Back in the bedroom, Eleanor sank down at the desk and instructed the child stretched out on the floor. "In the morning," she said, "I will rise at six o'clock, in time to read my devotional and get breakfast going. I will awaken you at six-thirty unless you bathe tonight, in which case you may sleep until seven. You will dress and set the table, and when we're finished eating, you will clear the dishes and wash or dry them, whichever you choose."

Abby stared at her silently.

"At a quarter of eight Harley Rae's daughter, Reenie, who is your age, will come by and walk with you to school."

"Can't we go in the car?"

"We will ride when it rains and when the temperature is low. The school is only a few blocks. You and Reenie will have time to get acquainted."

"What will I wear?"

"Whatever you wore to your own school. You needn't feel strange here. In a school as small as ours, you'll be the most important person there for the rest of the week. By the time the other students stop thinking of you as the new girl, you'll be as much at home as they are."

"Are you sure about that?"

"Very sure."

Abby went on with questions: Would she come home at noon? Who would give her lunch money? Eleanor answered approvingly. "It's important to know as much as you can about new surroundings no matter what age you are."

"I'll feel safer, won't I?"

"You will, Abigail." *Just as she and Abel had held fast to their own securities in that long-ago time before the planet shifted.* "Go ahead with your letter. I'll be in my room if you need anything."

"Do you have a little blanket? Like a baby's blanket? I left mine in Marshall."

"What did you sleep with last night?"

"My grandpa's wool shirt. I put it on."

Eleanor thought longingly of Abel's mackinaw wrapped around her, giving rise to the fragrance or scent or whatever it was that was Abel's alone. "I'll see what I can find."

Rummaging through a drawer, she came up with a soft pink shawl she remembered wearing to play lady when she was a child. "How about this?"

Abigail examined it. "It's a little long."

"You can fold it."

"Okay." She draped it across her shoulders as Eleanor had done at her age. "I like your house. Tomorrow can I go exploring?"

"You may. After you finish your homework."

"I do my homework after supper."

"Let's try doing it after school, while you are still in the school mode. Then you can do other things, and after supper you'll have time to read until you're sleepy." *Pray God*, thought Eleanor, *that our bedtimes coincide!*

"I'd rather watch TV. Except it's so green. Can't you get it fixed?"

"I'll see," said Eleanor. "If you feel hungry again before you go to bed, you may eat an apple from the bowl on the table."

"At home I ate cookies."

"Here we eat apples."

At the start of the next week Eleanor took a long breath and congratulated herself. No catastrophes had occurred, and the child seemed reasonably happy. She called Grace. "I'm better at this than I thought would be."

"Better at mothering?" Grace laughed as if remembering her own desperate days before her two raucous sons grew into fine men. "You're lucky, Eleanor. Abigail is a well-behaved little girl."

"I deserve credit too," Eleanor protested. "A maiden lady. No experience with children." She backtracked quickly. "Well, forty years. But in a different context."

The context, she mused after Grace had hung up, made all the difference. Living with a child bore little similarity to the student-teacher relationship.

As Abel had warned, she had lost her privacy. Not that Abigail poked her nose into places she shouldn't, but her presence in the house required that Eleanor shape up. She had to make herself presentable when she appeared for breakfast, make her bed every morning whether she felt like it or not, and forgo certain careless habits she enjoyed. Passing gas, for one. Leaving the bathroom door open and carrying on conversations with herself.

Most inconvenient of all was the constant kitchen duty. Snacks were expected, and regular meals. Eleanor was so often at the grocery store that the cashiers (her former students) had lost their awe of her and popped gum in her face and called her honey.

My life now, Eleanor thought uneasily, *must be something like being married. Bound up*, was the way she thought of it, *in another person's needs*.

Her own needs went largely unmet. In the late afternoons, when she walked over to the cottage, she rarely had a chance to be alone with Abel. Abigail was there, perched on a sawhorse chattering to her grandfather or racing through the rooms with Harley Rae's daughter, Reenie, a thin, big-eyed child who, unlike her grandmother Cleo, tended toward shyness.

"She's not shy with me," Abigail said one evening when she was helping with supper. "And not at school either." She looked at Eleanor. "I think it's you."

"Possibly it is," Eleanor said, gratified.

"Sometimes you're sort of prissy."

"*Dignified* is a more accurate term."

Abigail squinted up from the bowl of peas in her lap. "You're always kind of on a high horse."

Eleanor considered this possibility. "How would you prefer me to be?"

"Oh. Well. I like you all right the way you are. And Grampa does. And so does Miss Grace."

"But Reenie does not."

"I think she's scared of you."

Eleanor looked directly at her. "Are you scared of me?"

"I was, sort of, the first day I came. But I'm used to you now." The child returned the look. "Are you used to me?"

"I find it pleasant having you in my house, but I am not quite used to it."

"How much longer do you think it will it take?"

Eleanor heard the wistful tone of the child's voice. "Possibly a day more. Or maybe two."

"Grampa told me if I was wearing you out, I should come back to the trailer."

A longing for Abel overwhelmed Eleanor. "Your grandfather." She cleared her throat. "Is a considerate man." *Tender. Enduring.* She forced her thoughts away from the hours not spent with him since Abby's arrival, the close moments she had missed, the kisses.

She said to the child, "Actually, I think we're getting along very well. Wouldn't you say so?"

Abigail shelled peas. "Most of the time."

One Saturday Eleanor took Abigail shopping. "You need a nice church dress."

"A dress!" the girl said.

"Or a pretty skirt and blouse." They bought two shirts—a compromise—but when they were back in the car, Abigail voiced another objection.

"I don't like spending Grampa's money. It's nice enough of him to let me live with him without putting him in the poorhouse. Of course"—she scowled—"I'm not really living with him, I'm living with you. Are you paying for these things and my food and everything?"

"No," said Eleanor, moved by her concern. "But it's gracious of you to ask."

Abigail was quiet for a moment. "What does 'gracious' mean? Is it like in 'Oh, my gracious!'?"

"No. Used in this way, it means that you are thoughtful of other people's feelings, that you are kind and polite."

Eleanor put the car in gear and drove down Main Street. She stopped at the post office, but instead of getting out, she turned to Abigail. "What do you know about poorhouses?" She had not thought in years of the poor farms of her childhood.

"I don't know what they are exactly, but my mom says we have to watch it with our money or that's where we'll land, especially with my dad gone and her not working. You know she quit her good job because she thought if my dad knew he had to support us, he would get a better job. But he didn't. He went off. And then she couldn't get her old job back, and she doesn't want to be some flunky making half what she's worth."

"I see," said Eleanor, seeing quite clearly this aspect of Kit, mentioned by the father and reinforced by the daughter. "Would you like to get the mail, and then we'll go home?"

As they pulled into the garage, Abigail said, "Have you ever seen a poorhouse?"

"Once," said Eleanor.

"What was it like?"

"It was depressing. I was about your age, and my father wanted to speak with a man who lived at the poor farm, so we drove out there. I remember a row of unpainted houses and women sitting on the porches, staring at us as we drove by. The people who lived there were supposed to feed themselves with what they could raise in vegetable gardens and with chickens and so on, but the land wasn't fit for raising anything. The chickens, I recall, had hardly any feathers." Eleanor paused. "I felt very sorry for them."

Then in a brisker tone she said to the solemn child beside her, "Fortunately, we learned something in this country from that period in our history. Now we have government programs that help people through bad times and help them find work and suitable housing. Everyone needs to be sensible about making and spending money, but no one who is willing to put forth the effort to do his best and use his intelligence to help himself will ever have to worry about going to a poorhouse. I doubt very much whether he could even find one."

"So I can forget about that?"

"I believe you can."

Abigail sighed. "You were gracious to tell me."

19

One Monday toward the end of November, Grace called Eleanor over for tea.

"I had my tea with breakfast," Eleanor said, "but I wouldn't mind half an hour away from this house."

"Feeling confined?"

"Feeling trapped," said Eleanor. "Intellectually dead. Poisoned by domesticity. Smothered in motherhood."

"I'll put on the kettle."

Seated in Grace's living room in antimacassared chairs, a tea table between them and a gas heater warming their toes, Eleanor commented on an old upright piano whose finish had crackled: "Do you ever wonder how many generations of moths have hatched out of that instrument?"

"I keep mothballs in it!" Grace answered indignantly. "If you let the felts go, a piano is ruined."

"You don't play it anyway."

"I play it every Sunday! As you would know if you opened your windows."

"It's winter, Grace."

"There were twelve Sundays in summer. You could have heard it then."

"It's been a hundred years since we had summer."

Grace said sympathetically, "You're about to snap, aren't you? I saw in church yesterday how you were twitching around. Relax, Eleanor, and have a cookie."

"I don't want a cookie." But eventually she had two, and then reached for another. "Actually," she said when her cup was refilled, "considering the task I have undertaken, I'm doing quite well."

"It's very different, isn't it?" Grace sympathized. "When you were a teacher, you were through with children when the last bell rang."

"I think of that." Eleanor sighed. "But I was warned. Abel told me I'd lose my privacy if I took the child in."

"Is her nose in everything?"

"Not so much. It's just that she's there."

"Oh, I know. Sissy stayed with me when her baby brother was born. Two and a half weeks with my two kids and her. I thought I'd go crazy."

Eleanor blinked tiredly. "If I feel like sleeping late, I have to get up. When I go to the bathroom, I have to shut the door. I have twice as much laundry to do. I try not to snore—"

"Or belch," Grace offered. "I had a time with belching when Sissy was here. At the first slip-up you should have heard her shriek, *Aunt Grace!* As if she'd never heard Maggie belch when I know for a fact she takes a ton of Tums."

"I'm taking two tons."

They sat for a time watching leaves blow past the window.

"Do you think my life now is anything like being married?"

"Yes," said Grace, and then bethought herself. "Well, it is and it isn't. The difference, you see, is that in marriage there's a man."

"A man," said Eleanor, "would make it infinitely worse."

"Only on the first night."

"Grace!" said Eleanor.

"What I mean is. Well, on the wedding night. The woman isn't quite familiar with—being familiar."

"I was speaking of daily living!"

"I'm coming to that."

"Too slowly for me." Eleanor set her cup down sharply. "Let's drop it, shall we?"

"No, we shall not drop it! I have a point to make here."

"Then make it, for heaven's sake! I'm a busy woman."

"If you'd hold your horses, Eleanor, you might learn something!"

"*Grace!*"

"All *right!* Just listen a minute, will you? When the person who is around all the time is the man you love, you can be yourself. You can snore or pass gas or whatever you want because if you're going to spend the rest of your life with him, you can't always be shutting the bathroom door! You're *close*, don't you see? You're one person, Eleanor!"

Eleanor sent her a withering look. "If I were married for two lifetimes, I would never *not* shut the bathroom door!" She rose from her chair. "As for passing gas, I would explode first!"

"Sit down!" said Grace. "I'm not through talking."

"I'm through listening!"

"You haven't heard everything. Somewhere in this conversation I want a chance to tell you that I would like to give you a breathing space with Abigail!"

Eleanor halted at the door. "A breathing space?" She turned back to Grace. "What do you mean?"

"After school I want to teach her to sew."

"Sew!" said Eleanor. "That child? It would take forever."

"She's not you, Eleanor; she might enjoy sewing. And if she does, all the better for you. After she gets her lessons, she can come over every afternoon for a couple of hours. I'll take her to town and buy a pattern and we'll make her a dress."

"Every afternoon?" Eleanor sat again. "I'd have time to read." Tears filled her eyes. "I might find a few minutes to talk privately with Abel."

"Abel, I'm sure, would welcome that."

"Grace." Eleanor's voice cracked. "You've always been a good friend, but this—this charitable act, this sacrifice of your time—I'm overcome by your kindness. Your generosity."

"It's selfishness really," Grace confessed. "I only had boys. I never had a chance to teach a daughter to sew."

Eleanor moaned softly. "What can I do for you?"

"Let's see. You can bake me a lemon cake—or maybe a chocolate one—when you've caught up on your reading." Grace smiled. "And you can marry Abel."

Eleanor hurried home, bursting with eagerness to tell Abby about Grace's offer, but when the girl came in she dragged by without speaking and went to her room.

Eleanor called after her, "Shall we try that again?"

A sullen voice responded, "Try what?"

"Entering. Greeting me pleasantly. Possibly smiling."

Abby came out. "I don't feel like smiling."

"Then try entering and greeting."

"Do you mean for real?"

"I mean," said Eleanor, "for you to exit the room and reenter properly."

Abigail raised her voice. "Do you know what? I'm really tired of you! I'm tired of fig preserves every morning and sheets that smell like lavender. I'm tired of having to watch every minute so I don't do something wrong because you're so damned right all the time!"

Eleanor replied with absolute calm, "And you, Miss Abigail, are distressingly rude."

The child burst into tears.

Eleanor let her cry. She had spent much of her life drying children's tears. Often—especially after her parents had died—she had wished she were a child again, free to boo-hoo out her pain and relieve her sorrow.

"Come over here," she said when the outburst died down. "Let's sit at the table."

Abigail came reluctantly, still sobbing.

"Now tell me what it is."

"It's none of your business."

"If I were to guess, I'd say you're homesick."

"I am not homesick! How could I be homesick when I don't have a home?"

"You gave an address to the principal at school. You received letters from your grandfather at that address."

"A home has to have somebody in it!"

"Ah—you're right. A home is considerably more than a house, isn't it?"

In a muffled voice Abigail asked, "Why doesn't my mother call me?"

"There could be all kinds of reasons." Eleanor tried to think of one. "She may not have a phone. She may be short of money."

"My mother would have a phone if she had to sell the car!"

Quite likely, Eleanor thought. It takes a daughter to know a mother. To Abigail she said with quiet authority, "You haven't heard from your mother because she misses you so much she wouldn't be able to speak if she heard your voice."

Abigail looked up. "Do you really think so?"

"I really do." A small but necessary lie God would surely forgive.

"Mom does cry real easy. Like me, I guess."

"It's been my experience that women are the worst about missing their children."

Abigail sniffled. "Do you have a Kleenex?"

"I have a clean handkerchief." Eleanor fished in her pocket.

The girl brought it to her nose. "It has the same smell— scent—as those dresses in the closet."

A lump crowded Eleanor's throat. *Won't it be fine if we both break down!* She pushed back her chair. "Would you like something to drink? I have apple juice."

"In a minute," said Abigail, her voice still wobbly. "I have to go out and come in again."

"I think in this instance we will postpone doing that and get on with your snack. You get the juice. And I'll bring the cookies."

"Cookies?"

"Grace baked them this morning." Eleanor went to the cabinet and brought back the plateful Grace had sent home with her. "I'm glad she reminded me that sometimes we need cookies."

Abigail's eyes welled again. "I really miss my mom."

"Of course you do. I miss mine too."

"But yours is dead."

"Oh, yes. She died long ago."

Abby set down the juice pitcher and took a seat next to Eleanor.

"The circumstance is different," Eleanor said, "your missing your mother, who will be returning, and my missing mine, who won't, but the feeling is similar when a loved one is absent, whether dead or alive."

"I never thought about it like that."

"Because you've had no occasion to. But now you do have, and you have a new understanding."

Abigail sipped her juice. "What do you do when you miss your mother?"

"I sometimes cry. Or I write in my daybook. But more often than not, I welcome the memories of her because they bring her back to me, and I am close to her again, for a little while at least."

"I could do that, I guess."

"I'm sure you could, but there's nothing wrong with honest tears. Now," she said in a brighter voice, "I have a surprise. Miss Grace has offered to teach you to sew."

"To sew!" said Abby. "But I don't know how!"

Eleanor laughed, and then so did Abigail at her silly answer. "Do you mean sew on a sewing machine?"

"I presume so. She didn't say, but she did say she would like you to come over this afternoon after you've done your homework. She wants you to go with her to town and choose a pattern for a dress."

"A church dress." Abigail searched Eleanor's face. "She doesn't like those pants I've been wearing to church."

"I believe it's more that she would enjoy your company and the pleasure of teaching you to do something she loves."

"Sewing?"

"Yes. If you think you would like that."

The child scrambled up. "I did my homework at school. Can I go right now?"

"Yes. Yes, you may."

Abby rushed out and came back just as quickly. "Good-bye, Miss El!"

She went out, slamming the door hard enough to make the glass rattle.

20

Eleanor discovered that her afternoons off were a mixed blessing. She rested, but when she tried to read, she found that for the first time in her life she couldn't concentrate on fiction. Too much real life was swirling around her.

Abigail's schoolwork, for one thing. The child brought home papers with only mediocre grades and did not respond willingly to Eleanor's offers of help.

"I can get it," she said.

Eleanor was sure she could if she had any interest in getting it, but her mind was on her absent mother and on a home that was no longer home. Her study time was largely given over to childish drawings of boxy little houses that looked so much like the honeymoon cottage, they broke Eleanor's heart.

It was her place, Eleanor knew, to scold the girl, but how could she when so many of her own hours were spent daydreaming and gazing out windows at the winter starkness of trees against gray skies?

December. Year's ending. The strangest year of her life. The most exhilarating. The most frightening. Long ago, when grief subsided after her parents died, she had taken herself in hand and moved forward, but in her present situation the future she so urgently needed to glimpse remained cloaked in uncertainty. Unanswered questions marred every peaceful moment. *What would happen when the cottage was finished, as it soon would be? What would she do with the rest of her life if Abel said good-bye and drove away? And what if he stayed? What then?*

Since her outburst in the kitchen that had ended in Abel's quiet question: *What kind of husband would a man like that make?* there had been no further mention of marriage. They were adrift, Eleanor thought, on a shoreless sea, day following night, endlessly.

Abel loved her, she was certain of that, but roving was in his blood. He had never put down roots anywhere, he had said. If they did marry (as unlikely as such a possibility seemed), it would be up to her to compromise. In good conscience she could never try to tie him down against his will, though his absences would drive her crazy. Every day he was gone she would die a little, wondering where he was and if he would return. Could she stand up to that? Order in all things had always been her stronghold. She had built her life around practical thinking and dependable behavior. *Around stodginess,* her inner voice taunted, making her want to weep. But stodgy or not, she couldn't imagine herself surviving in a state of flux, of Abel coming and going without reason or purpose.

Still, if he were no longer with her, what would it matter if she survived or not?

Such distressing thoughts drove her one afternoon to break her rule of not interfering with Abel's work. She

needed to be near him, to absorb some of his calm, to re-
new her patience, which was almost at an end. Taking a
quick look at herself in the bathroom mirror, she hurried
through the thicket to the cottage.

Coming quietly into the kitchen, she expected to find
him somewhere else in the house, in the living room
maybe, touching up nicks in the paint, or in one of the
bedrooms, studying the tin ceiling he was preparing to
clean. But instead he was there, in the kitchen, sitting on
the sawhorse, *smoking a cigarette!*

"Abel Brown!"

"Eleanor!" He jumped to his feet.

"It's clear now why I had orders never to pop in!"

"Oh, glory." He looked at her helplessly. "It was just one
cigarette, just something I needed today to kind of quiet
down."

Eleanor stared. This was the man from whom she
sought calm!

He came forward, wearing a whipped-dog look. "Listen,
I haven't been doing this all along." He brought out a new
pack of cigarettes with only one missing. "It just happened
today."

"It *happened*? Those cigarettes fell out of the sky? How
would you feel if your granddaughter had caught you?"

"The same way I feel now. Like a fool, going backward
instead of forward." He went to the sink and ran water
over the cigarette. "You know I couldn't have been smoking behind your back." He laughed lamely. "You would
have sniffed me out in a minute with that nose of yours."

"I do not perceive that as a compliment!"

Abel sighed. "It wasn't one exactly. Just a statement of
fact—and a safeguard I'm thankful for." He dropped the

pack in a trash basket and stood close to her. "Let's forget it, okay?"

"I think you should explain why you needed so badly to 'quiet down' that you took up smoking again."

"It's something I've had on my mind, something I'm working through."

Her heart froze.

"Where is Abby?" he said, nuzzling her cheek.

She answered numbly, "Abigail is where she is every afternoon: sewing at Grace's."

"Will she be gone long enough for you to kiss me?"

"I'm not sure I want to with you smelling of smoke."

He opened his arms. "Come see if you want to."

The kiss took in considerable territory and chased every thought from Eleanor's head except the wonder of being in his embrace. "We're acting like we're forty years old," she said when she got her breath back.

"Let's try for thirty." He kissed her again, murmuring against her cheek when the kiss was over, "Craving cigarettes today was a poor second for craving you. We're never alone five minutes anymore."

"I know," said Eleanor.

"How long has Abby been here? Two or three years?"

"I think it's closer to four." They smiled wryly at their joke. "But she's a precious girl, Abel. And she's missing her mother terribly. Have you heard from Kit?"

"Not since that note with the postmark I couldn't read."

"Weeks ago."

He released Eleanor and shoved his hands in his pockets. "It beats all, doesn't it, dumping her child and going off without a trace."

"She knew you'd try to stop her if you knew where she was."

"I'd strangle her now if I could get hold of her."

"She gave no indication of when she'd be back?"

"She'll call, she said, when she finds Don. Which might be never."

They leaned against the counter, fingers entwined.

"He could be anywhere." It was an old conversation they'd had before, but unexpectedly Abel added a new dimension.

"Abby told me something yesterday about a canceled check cashed in a grocery store in Little Rock. Written by Don. She said Kit pulled it out of the bank statement, and the next day she took out after him."

"I don't imagine he hung around Little Rock after he wrote it."

"I'm hoping maybe he did. I'm hoping he got some kind of job. I'm hoping that check was an SOS saying if you love me, Kit, you better come and get me."

"That's disgusting, Abel! A grown man. A father! And not enough backbone to act like one."

"I'm praying he's a case of arrested development, not a finished product with no hope for improvement."

"Is there a possibility of that?"

"Anything is possible. Isn't that what your church teaches?"

"My church teaches faith with realism," Eleanor said sharply. "If you attended services now and then, you'd know that."

Abel turned her toward him. "Maybe I will after we're married."

Eleanor felt a rush of anger mixed with desperation. "Marriage," she said, "is an uncharted area we have not explored. It's not a subject to joke about, and this is hardly the time to broach it."

He regarded her pensively. "The way things are, Miss El, we have to take whatever time we can find."

She turned her face away, hiding tears of frustration. "Then we'll just have to wait."

"Until Abby goes home? Who knows when that will be?"

Hearing the weariness in his voice, she relented, took his face in her hands, and kissed his mouth gently. "All things work together for good."

He held her tightly. "I know I'm the one who put the quietus on the marriage question. I'm the restless one who picks up and goes away, who is not to be relied on. Who starts smoking again after fourteen years." He buried his face in her hair. "But I know, too, how dismal life is when you aren't close by."

The call came on a Thursday, to Abel, not to Abby. He walked over from the cottage and told Eleanor while Abigail was at Grace's.

"Kit did find Don in Little Rock, but it took her a while to track down the grocery store where he cashed the check. He was living right around the corner. In a dump, she said. She's been there with him trying to persuade him to come home. And he's finally agreed to."

"When?"

"In the next week or so, when he gets his paycheck."

"He has a job?"

"Some little something."

They were talking in the living room, where Eleanor had been sorting through a box of old photographs that lay scattered on the couch. "Are they coming for Abigail?"

Abel nodded, stacking the pictures on the lamp table so he could sit next to her. "But let's not tell her until we know for sure, in case they don't show up." He looked at Eleanor. "What's wrong? Aren't you glad?"

"I thought I'd be glad." Eleanor struggled with the clamor of mixed emotions. "I want very much for Abigail to be reunited with her family. But what about us? How will we feel after she's gone?"

"Empty. And relieved! We'll get back to where we were. Pick up where we left off."

And where is that? Eleanor longed to ask, but she said instead, "Abby's made a place for herself here. Having her with us has changed things."

"It hasn't changed how I feel about you."

Eleanor sat with her hands clutched in her lap, thinking suddenly about Christmas. The two of them celebrating together. Unless Abel went to Marshall. Or somewhere else. "You're nearly finished with the cottage," she forced herself to say. At her feet a known road fell away into dark crevasses. "You once said you might buy it. Are you still thinking of that?"

He pulled his chin. "Maybe I'll buy it." In another moment he said, "I'll have to ask my wife."

Eleanor blanched.

"After everything we've been through," he said quietly, "you *are* going to marry me, aren't you?"

He waited, his head to one side, his blue eyes watching her.

"Was that a proposal?" she finally whispered.

"I could get down on my knees, I guess. If you'll help me up." He took her hands in his. "Let me try it again.

"Miss El," he said, "would you do me the great honor of changing your name to Brown-Bannister?"

"Bannister-Brown." Her whole body trembled. "Do you really think we can do that, Abel? Get married? Be husband and wife here at the end of our lives? It isn't reasonable."

"It isn't, thank God. It's foolish and reckless and whatever you want to call it, but it's what we want, what I want."

She closed her eyes. "I want it too. I want it so much that if you hadn't asked me, I would have asked you. I would have run after your trailer if you drove away." Her voice broke. "I would have chased you to Little Rock."

"As long as I live I'll love you, Eleanor."

Encircled in his arms she lost track of pitfalls and miseries, of whatever might lie ahead. The practicalities, the niggling fears that woke her in the night and tormented her during the day, buzzed away like mosquitoes. But when he let her go, they swarmed in again.

Abel smoothed her forehead. "What are you thinking?"

She said after a moment, "I'm trying to make it all fit."

He said, "Take your time, my dear." *As if he were promising that he wasn't going anywhere?*

She held one of his hands, stroking the back of it, the scars and bumpy places, the veins standing up. "For so long I've known myself as a single woman. As a spinster, Abel. I am asking myself now, who is this woman you want to marry?"

"I can tell you who she is," he answered without hesitation. "She's mine. Her contradictions, her ups and downs, her dignity, her girlishness. All belong to me. She's the crown of my life, and I will cherish her forever."

She brought his hand to her cheek. "That was beautiful. Eloquent."

He kissed her again, gently on her brow, then on her mouth.

"Abel, you realize, don't you, that I may never get over being a spinster?"

"You don't have to be afraid, Eleanor, of anything."

"I am afraid." She laid her head against his chest. "Except when you're kissing me. Then I'm appalled at how wanton I am."

He brought up her chin, his eyes twinkling. "We should get married right away. Before we get in trouble."

They spent a while holding each other, murmuring little things, laughing like children.

Then Eleanor said, "I'd like to spend our first night in the honeymoon cottage."

"How about the first year?"

A year, she thought. *Can we have a year together before you set out again?*

"It's our time now to do whatever we want, whenever we want to."

Even if it only lasts a week, she thought, *I will have had that week.* "How soon will you be finished with the work?"

"Bill's coming Saturday morning, and Dudley, as soon as he gets away from the store. We should wrap it all up if we work both days, Saturday and Sunday—if you'll let us work on the Sabbath."

"This Sunday you may. But next Sunday you'll have to be in church."

He shifted on the couch. "We'll see. When the time comes."

"If you're not there, Abel, I'll be left waiting at the altar."

Anticipating his shock, she went on quickly. "Didn't you just say we ought to get married right away? Or do you want a big wedding? We'll have to wait until spring if we have a big wedding. You'll have to rent a tuxedo. I'll have to have invitations printed and send them out. Is that what you want?"

"I just want to get married!"

"Then the less fuss the better."

He grinned widely. "You've been thinking about this."

"It's best to prepare for eventualities. Even if they never materialize."

Pleased as a boy he said, "If you'll buy the paint, Miss El, I'll print in boxcar letters on the front of the church, 'THIS SUNDAY: EVENTUALITY MATERIALIZING!'"

"Do that and *you'll* be left waiting at the altar!"

He laughed. "Tell me what else has been going through your head."

She took her time getting into it, relishing the details. As soon as the cottage was finished, she said, they would begin moving in. Her things and his.

"Into your room and mine?"

She glanced away. "But we can't move everything." She pointed out the full bookcases, the wind-up phonograph, two huge old chairs. "Just the contents of this room would fill up the cottage. We'll have to be selective. Like young people starting out who don't have much."

"Who don't need much." Abel squeezed her shoulder. "Except each other."

"I'll take a few things from my kitchen over there. And you can do the same." Her excitement mounted. "The trailer and this house will be places we can go when we want a change of scenery. You can come over here and play the violin."

"I may take up my horn again."

"Lovely," she said. "You can practice here while I'm over there."

He gave her a smacking kiss, and she tapped his cheek lightly. "I haven't told you about the wedding."

"By all means, let's hear it."

"We will attend the Sunday service, and after the last song, the minister will announce that Miss Eleanor Bannister and Mr. Abel Brown will be joined in holy matrimony following the benediction. All who choose may stay as witnesses, and afterward there will be coffee and cake in the fellowship hall. I'll have Grace stand up with me, and you could have—"

"Bill." He grinned. "I've been thinking too."

"I'll ask Harley Rae to make the cake and Cleo to cut it. I think she'll be pleased."

Eleanor paused to catch her breath. "And I would like Abigail to be the flower girl with a little basket of blossoms to strew in front of us as we go out."

Abel's look softened. "Abby may be gone."

"Well, she can't be! You'll just have to telephone them, Abel! Your daughter and your granddaughter should be here for your wedding. Kit and Don can arrange it if they want to. I pray they will want to."

Abel gazed at her earnest face. "I'll phone tonight."

"Listen! Abby's coming!"

They heard her calling back to Grace, "See you tomorrow!"

"What shall we tell her, Abel?"

"Let's not mention Kit and Don since we don't know for sure."

"Or the wedding either. It's too soon, don't you think? We've barely decided."

The kitchen door opened, and Abigail called in an excited voice, "You're here, aren't you?"

"In the living room," Eleanor answered.

The child came rushing in, cheeks red, a huge smile on her face. "Look at this!" She held out her dress, finished just enough so they could see how it would look with the buttons sewn on and the hem in. A light blue dress with sprigs of white flowers.

"It's going to have lace around the collar!"

"And this is your work?" Abel reached for it.

"It's not all my work. Miss Grace helped a little. Mostly when I had to rip out. And with the cutting and all. The machine sewing I did myself."

"It's beautiful," said Eleanor, taking it from Abel to examine it carefully. "You can be proud of this."

"I wish I could show my mother!"

"She'll see it," said Abel. Then hastily, "A dress like this will last a long time."

Abby's joy faded. "Is it going to be a long time before I see her?"

"Not so long you can't stand it, Abby."

She leaned against his knee. "She's been gone forever. It's like she forgot me. I may not can stand it."

Abel looked at Eleanor who was looking back at him.

"Do you think—?" she said.

"Yes." He nodded. "Part of it anyway."

"Abby," said Eleanor, "we have something to tell you."

Alarmed, Abby drew back. "What? What is it?"

"You've made such a lovely dress," Eleanor said gently. "Would you do your grandfather and me the honor of wearing it at our wedding?"

21

Abigail was so taken with the idea of Eleanor and Abel actually getting married that she could scarcely eat the supper Eleanor put together for the three of them.

"I'm going to be in the wedding! I'm going to wear my dress and be in the wedding!"

"So is Miss Grace," Abel told her, trying to promote calm, but Eleanor could see in his eyes the same rampant joy that was crowding her chest.

"I'm hoping Grace will stand up with me," she explained, smiling at Abigail, then at Abel again.

"Stand up?" the child questioned. "What do you mean?"

"Grace will stand beside me and hold my bouquet while we take our vows. Grace will be my matron of honor."

"What will I be?"

"The flower girl," said Abel. "You'll go in front of us out of the church. What's that word, Eleanor, for what she'll be doing?"

"Strewing," said the bride-to-be.

"Strewing." He grinned. "You'll be strewing flower petals out of a basket onto the carpet."

"And I'll be wearing my dress! Let's go now and tell Miss Grace!"

"If we do that," said Eleanor, "she won't sleep all night. Tomorrow afternoon when you go over to sew, I'll go with you and you may tell her then."

"I can't wait to see her face! Her mouth will fly open the way it did in the store when I told her I'd never owned a dress before. She'll say, 'Oh my stars!' And then she'll cry."

"Cry?" said Abel.

"Because she'll be so happy. I asked her in the store when we were buying my pattern, did she think you and Miss El would ever get married, and she said, 'I pray every night they will.'" Abigail's eyes sparkled. "She said something else too."

"What?" said Abel.

"I can't tell you, it's too silly."

"You brought it to our attention," Eleanor said. "You are obliged to tell us."

"Obliged?"

"It is your responsibility to pass on this information."

"Well. Miss Grace said—" A fit of giggling delayed the revelation. "Miss Grace said you were made for each other!"

"What's silly about that?"

"Grampa! Think of all the ladies in Texas. And Louisiana and Arkansas! You would have picked one of them if you hadn't stopped here, if the storm hadn't put a hole in Miss El's roof."

Abel looked at Eleanor. "But I did stop here. That's the point."

"Eat your supper, Abigail," Eleanor urged. "It's almost bedtime."

The child sighed. "I don't think I can sleep either. If it's going to be on Sunday morning, will we have to sit through church before we have it? Why don't we have it on Saturday?"

"Sunday makes it simpler. Our friends will already be there."

"Oh, I see. When Reverend Philbin stops preaching we'll get up like we're leaving, only instead we'll go up to the front and have a wedding!"

"Exactly," said Eleanor.

"And everyone who thinks it's just a plain old Sunday will be so surprised!"

"If you don't tell it all over," Abel said.

"I can tell Reenie, can't I?"

"No," said Eleanor.

"I'll make her cross her heart!"

"If you're busting to talk about it," Abel said, "talk to Miss Grace."

Abigail turned to Eleanor. "What will you wear? Miss Grace could sew you a wedding dress! She wouldn't have much time, but she could do it, I bet."

"I'm thinking about a dress I already have."

Abel was about to remind her that she had emptied her closet for Harley Rae's sale, but Abigail broke in, "Tell me again what the flower girl does." It was obvious she remembered every word Abel had said concerning her part, but it was so delicious to think about that she wanted to hear it again. "Will I carry rose petals?"

"Rose petals would be nice."

"And daisies," said Abel. "A first-class wedding has to have daisies."

"I thought I might carry blue delphinium and white stock." Eleanor smiled. "But I think white daisies will be even prettier."

Abel wore such a look of absolute contentment it brought a lump to her throat and a surge of gratitude that he hadn't chosen a bride in Louisiana—or Arkansas!

"People will catch on when I come in with my basket," Abigail said. "And you'll be wearing your wedding dress. They'll want the wedding to be right away and skip the sermon."

"It'll be a challenge all right," Abel said, "not to wiggle around and want to get on with it."

"I think Reverend Philbin will preach something especially for us, so we will need to pay attention."

Abigail groaned.

"The whole day will be our wedding day," Eleanor said, her face flushed. "Every moment will be important. Every second will have its own place. I intend to notice everything and remember it always."

"Well, I think it's terrible my mother won't be there!"

"There's still time to hear from her," Abel soothed. "In the meantime, try to enjoy thinking about that possibility. If she doesn't make it, we'll at least have had the happiness of hoping she might."

"I want her *really* to be here!"

"We all want that," Eleanor said. "Now, finish your supper and go take your bath. When you wake up tomorrow, you'll be one day closer to wearing your dress."

"And strewing my rose petals!"

22

By early afternoon the Saturday before the wedding, the cottage was ready for the next evening's occupancy by the bride and groom. Abel, finished with his work, had gone to the barbershop, and Abigail and Reenie were at the movies.

Eleanor, wandering in the silence of the cottage, said without enthusiasm, "Alone at last. Time to do whatever I please."

But what was there to do? Every room was in order. Her wedding dress was pressed and hanging in a closet in the old house. The flowers were ordered. The cake was made.

She looked about, breathing unsteadily—*perspiring,* for heaven's sake!

Eleanor Bannister, she scolded, *you have time now to read! Every troubling matter is settled. With nothing to distract you, you can lose yourself in a book and, before you know it, regain your composure.*

From the shelf in the living room she took down an old favorite and settled on the couch—familiar, comforting. In the soft cushions, the imprint of Abel's body sat beside her in the spot he had occupied before going off to town. A pillow, mashed by his elbow, nudged her own.

She read a few lines and thought of Abel, wondering if he had remembered to polish his shoes. Down a few more lines she lost sight of the printed page. In its place, she saw herself, rising from the church pew, her bouquet trembling for everyone to see.

She had never fainted. But she had never been married before either!

At the last minute Abel might not show up.

She might back out herself. *Elderly bride runs from church.*

She slammed the book shut. "How can I concentrate on Jane Eyre when my own life is more than I can cope with!" The very *idea* of reading made her sick. At lunch she had felt sick, smelling tuna salad. And now the smell of fresh paint had set her head spinning. *A younger bride as sick as I am would probably be pregnant!* She thanked God there was no chance of that. But in the next breath she remembered that only hours from now she would be facing the intimacy that produced pregnancy.

She fled the room, dreading Abel's return, yet desperately needing it.

In the last hectic week, he had been her steadying point, strolling calmly through the cottage in his overalls, seeing to final details and catching her by the waist to kiss her whenever he could delay the antlike trips she was making between houses with the things she couldn't live without.

She and Abel had begun the transfer by selecting pieces of furniture that would be suitable for the cottage.

The couch first, and then Eleanor had chosen the bed that had always been hers. Abel's choice was one with a carved headboard, gargoylish enough to produce nightmares, but since Eleanor had no intention of sleeping in it, she kept quiet.

The kitchen table and chairs and the smaller pieces they readily agreed on, but Abel especially wanted the big leather chair of her father's in the living room.

"It will look ridiculous," Eleanor told him, unable this time not to voice an opinion. "It's out of scale for the cottage."

Abel said, "Did your father care about scale when he came home after work and stretched out in it?"

"He didn't have it in the honeymoon cottage. I remember when he bought it and put it in the very spot it's in now."

"It's time, then, to put it in a new spot."

Eleanor thought not, but a few days later she was glad she had offered no further objection when she found herself unable to leave behind her outsized bedroom desk. Desk and chair went along with the other things that Abel and Dudley and Bill Taylor transported in their trucks.

After the two helpers left and the desk was situated in her small bedroom—the leather chair in the tiny living room—Eleanor noted wearily, "They look like zoo animals about to break out."

Abel said, "What does it matter? We're not decorating for *House Beautiful*. Whatever suits us is what we want."

She did feel pleased that her old desk, and the chair too, were accompanying her into married life. At that point, she had made up her mind to accept their awkwardness in their new setting, but now, in the agitated state in which she left the living room, she felt the leather chair on its brown haunches glaring at her threateningly.

In her bedroom, the desk in its corner monstrously dwarfed everything else. In spite of her determination to say no more, to *think* no more about it, it was obvious that she would always regard the chair and the desk as out of place in the cottage. *And herself as well?*

She stood still, her skin burning. Women reacted like this when they were having breakdowns! Silly, unreliable women, as far removed from herself as Tasmania from Texas.

She vowed, lips barely capable of movement, *I will not break down! I will not disgrace myself hours before my wedding! I will take hold of myself as I did when my parents died and stop this nonsense!*

Then she groped her way to the telephone.

Grace answered on the fourth ring. "Call back later. I'm setting my hair."

"Grace!" Eleanor pleaded. "I need to talk to you."

"Well, make it short. Wet hair is dripping down my back. I'm losing all my setting lotion!"

"Come over here. Please!"

"Now? I can't possibly come now. I have to finish what I'm doing or I'll look a fright tomorrow. Maybe I will anyway. I should have gone to the beauty parlor. I knew I should have."

"Grace, I need to talk to you. I need you to come over here before Abel gets back."

"Why?" Grace said, suddenly alarmed. "What's the matter? Have you spilled something on your wedding dress? Or torn it? If you've torn it, Eleanor, I don't know what in the world we'll do. That cloth is too fragile to stand five minutes more of fooling with."

"This is a more serious matter than a torn dress!"

"On the eve of your wedding? I can't imagine what. But I'll be there as soon as I can. Oh, wait—where are you?"

"At the cottage. Hurry." Eleanor hung up, staring blankly out the window at the shell driveway and the bare elm tree beside it.

All her life she had wanted to live in this cottage, had imagined herself in the doll-like paradise of its neat little rooms with someone at her side who must have been Abel. How dreadful to discover so tardily that she could never be at home here, that she didn't recognize herself here! She could give away her clothes every day of the week and still be entombed in the mold Miss Eleanor Bannister had made for herself, the concrete she was set in. Encroaching senility— or an absurd grasping at youth—had made her imagine she could alter herself, move over here and *become a wife*.

Grace called from the kitchen door, "Yoo-hoo! Where are you?"

"In my bedroom." Only it wasn't her bedroom. It never would be.

Grace, a towel on her head, came bubbling in. "If I catch my death of cold, it will be worth it just to look at that kitchen before you mess it up. It's beautiful! Everything is beautiful."

Eleanor turned a taut face toward her. "Grace, I don't belong here."

"What? You don't belong here?"

"I don't fit in here. I belong in my house beyond the thicket."

Grace gaped. "You've had a stroke, haven't you?"

"I've come to my senses." Eleanor paced around the room. "I've waked up from my dream. You're my friend. Why didn't you tell me what a fool I was making of myself?"

"Eleanor Bannister! You've been tippling. You've gotten into some of that Christmas wine!"

"I have not been drinking."

"It's understandable if you felt like you needed a little nip. It's a special day." Grace paused to eye her warily. "But if you haven't had a drink or two, I'm calling the doctor. Or Abel. Where is he?"

"You mustn't tell Abel anything about this!"

"It's his place to be here if you're having delusions."

"This is not a delusion. It is an absolute fact: I cannot get married."

Grace sat on the bed. "If this isn't goofy! Why on earth can't you?" She leaned forward suddenly. "It's that first wife of his. She's come back, hasn't she?"

"She's dead, Grace."

"You never said she was dead! And look at you, pale as death yourself! You better tell me exactly what the trouble is. We have to get you straightened out before tomorrow."

Eleanor shuddered. "When I agreed to marry Abel, I believed I could be something that I can never be. It's as simple as that: I took a step in the wrong direction."

"You took a step all right, up to your eyebrows! You can't back out now! *Tomorrow* is the wedding! The flowers, the cake—what's to become of them? And what about Abigail and her new little dress? She'll cry her eyes out if she can't be the flower girl." Grace caught her breath. "And what about Abel? Have you thought about him?"

Eleanor felt as if a bear had sat down on her chest. "Abel," she said.

"You love him, don't you?"

"I do love Abel." She wilted in the desk chair. "But if I marry him under false pretenses, I'll make him miserable."

"More miserable than he'll feel if you tell him you're calling it off?" Grace picked up a corner of the quilt covering the bed and fanned herself. "This is the most selfish thing I've ever heard of!"

"It's dishonorable. I know that, but I could never get up in that church tomorrow and commit myself to an unknown arrangement. To marriage, Grace!" Eleanor's voice rose shrilly. "Do you know what a serious step marriage is?"

Grace smiled suddenly. "How do your knees feel?"

"My *knees!* Grace! You're supposed to be helping me!"

"Tell me how they feel."

"Like—like boiled noodles," Eleanor stammered.

"And the back of your neck? Any prickles there?"

"I'm prickling all over! And besides that I'm sick at my stomach."

"And your palms, how are they?"

"If it makes the slightest difference, they're as wet as dead fish!"

Grace nodded happily, "It's *nerves*, you silly girl. You've got a bad case of bride jitters. And no wonder too, over here by yourself with nothing to think of except all the wrong things."

"Bride jitters!" Eleanor shrieked. "You oversimplify everything! You always do."

"Well, if you want to make a big case of it, go ahead, but I'm telling you, Eleanor, that's all that's the matter with you. You've got cold feet. And cold feet will pass if you grit your teeth and go on."

"I'd prefer to die than go through with this."

"I know about that, how the jitters slip up on you and hit you over the head. Before my first baby was born," Grace said chattily, "—that's Tom, you know, the veterinarian—I was eating chocolate ice cream and all of a sudden pure terror took hold of me. I told my mother, 'I can't go through with it. I want out!'" I said. "And my mother said to me, 'So does the baby.' Do you get the picture, Eleanor?"

"I'm calling off a wedding, not having a baby!"

"It's the same thing, don't you see? They both scare you to death. You don't know what's ahead, and you lose your confidence. Isn't that how you feel, fresh out of confidence?"

"I can't describe how I feel."

"You did a pretty good job a minute ago, good enough for me to see what the trouble is. And I'll tell you something else: a pregnant woman's got to go through with it, no matter what, but a bride has a choice. Only Eleanor, you've already made the choice. You decided to marry Abel because you love each other. You took your time coming to that decision, and that's what you have to do with marriage, take your time."

"I'm *scared*, Grace!"

"Sure you are. And so is Abel. You can count on that. Scareder than you, maybe, because he's been through it once and it didn't pan out. But scared or not, he's going to try it again. You owe him something for that, Eleanor, for loving you enough to give it another go."

Eleanor blinked back tears. "It's possible, Grace, that I have seriously undervalued you."

"You have. For years. But I don't hold it against you."

Eleanor wiped her eyes. "Why don't you, Grace?"

"Because I know it's hard on you to have a nosy friend who talks a lot and is sometimes silly." Grinning, she hoisted herself from the bed. "But to tell you the truth, Ellie, I've put up with you because I couldn't stand not to be around when you pulled off your next stunt."

Eleanor moaned. "Oh, Grace."

"Are you all right now?"

"I'm much better, thanks to you and your horse sense. I appreciate, Grace, that you came over here in the middle of your shampoo."

"Could I ask you a question before I go?"

"If it's about our separate bedrooms, the answer is no."

"I wouldn't dream of asking that. Not today anyway. Just tell me if you've heard anything from Abigail's mother."

"Nothing since the telephone call." Eleanor brought out a handkerchief and patted her damp brow. "Abel tried to call her back and let her know about the wedding, but the number she gave him was a pay phone in a grocery store. The woman who finally answered did know Kit and Don, but she said they had gone, had been gone for days."

"It doesn't take days to get here from Little Rock."

"They might have gone by Marshall to see about their house."

Grace said glumly, "If her mother doesn't make it here in time for the wedding, Abigail is going to be broken-hearted."

"Abel too." Eleanor had watched him working himself up to tell Kit that her Uncle Jim was her real father. And if he got through that, he said, he wanted to talk to her about her marriage and her child.

Eleanor had advised him to wait until another time. "She'll have shock enough when she finds out you're getting married."

"Good," Abel answered with rare bitterness. "She's shocked me more than once."

"That's vengeful, Abel!"

"Eleanor," he said, "can't you forget for five minutes that you're a Presbyterian?"

As Grace was leaving, the truck turned into the driveway. Abel met them in the kitchen. "Ladies," he said, "how is everything going?"

"Fine!" said Grace. "And you've got a nice haircut."

"I've been to the florist's too." He smiled at Eleanor. "I wanted to make sure they get your bouquets and Abby's basket situated on the front pew while folks are in Sunday school."

"And the altar flowers?" Eleanor asked, shaken still but feeling joy rising again inside her at the sight of him.

"They're taking them to the church at ten o'clock."

Eleanor turned to Grace. "We've sworn Alice at the flower shop to secrecy. And Harley Rae too, and Cleo, of course."

"You don't really think Cleo can keep a secret, do you? Besides that," said Grace, fidgeting with her head wrap, "the whole neighborhood has been glued to their windows watching the move."

Abel intervened. "Dudley and Bill Taylor have spread the word that Eleanor has decided to furnish the cottage." He squeezed her shoulder. "So I think we're safe with our big surprise."

Grace hurried to the door. "Excuse me, but I forgot something on the stove."

"Don't forget your hair," Eleanor called after her.

"Pretty quick exit," Abel commented.

"Because she's told someone," Eleanor replied, frowning. "If she's told Sissy, the whole town will know."

He put his arms around her. "It'll be all right, won't it, if they do?"

"It won't be what I planned," Eleanor fretted.

"But we'll get married just the same."

She leaned her head against his chest. "I got frightened after you left. Thinking about everything, I went into a tailspin. Grace came over and helped me out."

He kissed her forehead. "The barber helped me."

Eleanor pulled back. "You told him about the wedding?"

"Of course not, Eleanor. He lulled me into a good nap, going on about baseball."

23

Eleanor woke to dawn shadows cloaking the bedroom, blurring the shape of an unfamiliar bureau, a closet standing open in the wrong place. *Her wedding day*. It was fitting somehow that she should begin it in a room not her own.

For a brief period in her childhood, this room where she had been sleeping since the dismantling of her bedroom had been occupied by her mother's cousin, who suffered from somnambulism. One night on a walk he had awakened suddenly and banged into a lamp, which crashed against the door and cut a gash, not in his head, thankfully, but in the paint.

In the dim morning light, Eleanor could see that the scar was still there. Poor Cousin Hurley, outlived by a scratch on a painted board. Except for her, all were dead who might have remembered his affliction and his embarrassment the next morning when he confessed to his accident.

On some future day no one will be left to remember Eleanor Bannister: the bride who got married with one foot in the grave and the other on a banana peel.

Smiling, Eleanor turned on her side and thought of Abel's return yesterday. The mere sight of him had restored her to herself. Restless Abel, who had threatened to bolt at any minute, had stayed steady, and the solid Miss Bannister had melted into a puddle, been resurrected by Grace and brought back to life by Abel standing there in the hall, not driving down the highway pulling his trailer, running away as she, Eleanor the Invincible, had almost done.

Humbled, she reached for her daybook, remembering only then that the daybook had already made its transition and lay in a drawer of the desk that reigned supreme beyond the thicket. That she could have made such a fuss over the desk and her father's chair was inconceivable this morning, of no more importance than the missing daybook, which she seldom wrote in now. She was too tired at the end of a day looking after Abigail, and anyway, most of her thoughts she had already shared with Abel. The few thoughts she kept to herself were too private to put on paper and leave for someone to read later and embarrass her—even beyond the pale!

Abigail opened the door quietly and tiptoed in. "Are you awake, Miss El?"

"Fully awake."

"May I get in the bed?"

"This one time only."

Abigail snuggled in. "Are you excited?"

"I am. And you?"

"I've been awake a long time thinking of everything. Do you think I'll be scared strewing my flowers?"

"Certainly not. You'll be too happy to be frightened. The human body cannot entertain two strong emotions at the same time."

"Is that really true?"

"Would I tell you a falsehood?"

"My mother isn't coming, is she?"

Eleanor's heart hurt. "She may come."

"No, she won't."

"Move over here, Abigail. Lie next to me."

The child cried. "I wanted her to be here. I prayed she would be here."

"Let's try to remember what your grandfather said. We have had the pleasure of imagining her here to see you in your dress, to see her father married. If that's all we have, we have had that at least."

"It isn't enough. Where will I sleep tonight? Who's going to take care of me?"

"You have three people who love you taking care of you. You'll sleep at Miss Grace's while your grandfather and I get used to each other, and then we'll work out a plan for you to come back to us. Now I think we should get up and start this day."

"The day you want to notice everything and remember it forever."

"Yes," said Eleanor. "And you should do the same. Every day is precious, a brief life in itself that will never be repeated."

"Did you make that up?"

"I learned it, growing old." Eleanor pulled on her wrapper. "The trouble is, I'm forever forgetting it."

Abigail began smoothing the bed covers. Touched, Eleanor helped her. This moment, she thought, I *will* remember.

"Could I see your dress?"

Eleanor had showed it to no one except Grace, who had put in a few tucks here and there and invisibly mended the places time had damaged. She thought it more fitting for the groom to see it first, but looking into his granddaughter's face, she said, "Sit by the window and I'll try it on for you."

She went into the big closet, where her father's rowing machine was stored, and removed her nightgown, slipping the dress over her naked body.

The dress was one of her mother's, a champagne-colored silk, simply made, with long sleeves and falling from a loose waist in flowing panels that nearly met the floor. Her neck (her scrawny neck! she had lamented to Grace) was hidden by a high lace collar. More lace came down in a V that fastened onto the bodice with tiny pearl buttons.

"Of course I don't have on my shoes," Eleanor said, reentering the room, "but you'll have an idea of how I will look when I have my flowers and my hair is combed."

Abigail said, "We should have invited the whole town to see how beautiful you are!"

Eleanor swirled the skirt. "I always loved this dress when my mother wore it to parties in the evening with my father. It's held up well."

"It looks brand new—except it looks better than new. It looks—I don't know—like it *should* look for marrying Grampa."

Eleanor turned away, her throat too full to reply.

"What is Miss Grace wearing?"

"A church dress she's worn before," Eleanor managed to say. "Not new, not old, but very suitable."

Abigail shivered with excitement. "Let's go wake up Grampa!"

"Let's eat our breakfast," Eleanor said. Abel might like to spend his last morning in his trailer alone. "Afterward we will truly get dressed. I want to be seated in the church before Sunday school is over so that when people come in they will see only our backs."

"We could even skip breakfast. We could get dressed and go now!"

24

At ten-thirty sharp, Abel drove Eleanor and Abigail to Grace's house, where he got out and escorted Grace in her "not new but suitable" dress back to Eleanor's car.

Getting behind the wheel again, he said, "Not one, not two, but three beautiful ladies. How about that?"

"How about you, Grampa, you look beautiful yourself."

"You do," said Eleanor. It was her first time to see him in a suit. A far cry he looked from the string-bean man wearing a cap.

"I'm shaking, I'm so thrilled!" Grace said. "The last time I was maid of honor in a wedding was in 1949. I wore yellow shantung and looked like a banana going down the aisle."

"Miss Grace," said Abigail, "how does my dress look?"

"It couldn't be prettier." Grace gave her a hug. "Blue is certainly your color."

The church came into view. A few cars were parked alongside the building, but no one was moving in or out.

"Perfect," said Eleanor, hurrying them into the foyer to hang their coats on pegs before taking their seats in the first two rows of the sanctuary.

"The flowers *are* here!" Abigail exclaimed, charmed by her basket, bringing it close to Eleanor's nose.

"Summer Roses in December." Eleanor smiled, as thrilled as Grace. Her own bouquet of dwarf delphinium stems and white daisies lay in her lap, complimenting the champagne softness of her skirt.

She reached around to give Grace her bouquet and saw that the best man had arrived and seated himself beside the matron of honor.

"Good morning, Mr. Taylor. So good of you to come." Her face heated. *What a stupid thing to say! Of course he had come.*

"Well, Bill!" Abel said, turning around. "You do us right proud with that fancy tie around your neck."

"All slicked down," he whispered to Eleanor as they faced the front again. "A different-looking fellow from the one at our house on moving day."

The artist, thought Eleanor. He had transformed her ancient sink into a thing of beauty. Wouldn't it be interesting if he meant now to transform himself into a suitor! Too bad she hadn't noticed if his lips measured up to Grace's memory of the butcher's at Four Star.

A stirring began in the back of the church: shuffling feet, coughing, a smattering of chatter as the worshipers filed in.

And kept filing in!

Alarm fluttered in Eleanor's chest. There was entirely too much noise for a regular Sunday. She risked a quick glance over her shoulder.

"Oh, my lord."

"What is it?" whispered Abel.

"The church is almost full!"

"That's good, isn't it?"

"It is not good!" She took another quick look and picked out two of her former students with their families and an old school friend she hadn't seen in a hundred years.

Organ music began. The Reverend Philbin took his place at the pulpit. When the congregation rose to sing the first hymn, a great chorus of voices assaulted the ceiling. There was a scraping of chairs being brought in to accommodate the crowd.

"Abel," whispered Eleanor. "We won't have enough cake!"

He patted her hand. "It's all right, Miss El. It'll all work out."

Through gritted teeth she said, "When we get out of here, I am going to kill Grace."

She fell silent after that, too stunned to be aware of anything except impending disaster. The subject of the Reverend Philbin's sermon went over her head. If Abigail wiggled, she didn't know it. Finally she found herself standing for the benediction, rigidly awaiting the minister's announcement of the spoiled surprise.

"You are all invited to remain for the joining together in holy matrimony of Miss Eleanor Bannister and Mr. Abel Brown." The Reverend smiled beneficently. "And to partake afterward of the covered-dish dinner to be served in their honor in the fellowship hall."

Covered-dish dinner! Eleanor gasped.

Abel took her arm and led her to the altar. A quivering Grace appeared at her side, holding Abigail's hand. Mr. Taylor stood opposite, just behind Abel.

Beneath her breath, Eleanor murmured, "Who in the world would think of a covered-dish dinner for a wedding reception!"

"Friends," Abel whispered. "Kind, loving friends."

More words were spoken by the Reverend Philbin.

"I do," said Eleanor at the appropriate time. Abel kissed her, and then Abigail, with great decorum, strewed her rose petals down the aisle.

"Now, Miss El, wasn't that nice?" Abel said when the last guest had wished them well and ambled out, stuffed with food prepared by the finest cooks in town.

"It was wonderful. Extraordinary." Tears stood in her eyes. "But no one was surprised except me."

Grace said at her elbow, "I'm sorry about that, Eleanor."

"You needn't be. Your plans exceeded mine in every respect—but you did have your nerve, didn't you!"

Grace sighed. "I knew you'd take it wrong, me changing up things, but word got around and everyone who ever knew you wanted to be here."

"And *was* here!" said Eleanor. "Even two waitresses from the pizza café. But I was ready to kill you, Grace, when that crowd streamed in."

"You're over it, aren't you?"

"I am now, but in the sanctuary I couldn't think of anything except Harley Rae's cake, baked for thirty-five."

Harley Rae approached, looking triumphant but tired.

"Oh, my dear," said Eleanor, "only crumbs are left, but your cake was a masterpiece."

"I was proud to bake it for you, Miss Bannister. Mrs. Brown, I should say. But when Miss Grace said we'd have to have six layers, I stayed awake a few nights wondering what I'd do when they collapsed on the table."

"You needn't have worried. They stood up like a turreted castle."

"Thank you, and thank you too for asking my mother to cut the cake." Harley Rae's eyes glistened. "It's made her too shy to come over and tell you how much it pleased her."

"The pleasure was mine," said Eleanor. "I have always loved Cleo."

It was true, she realized. Earnest, gangling Cleo bent over her beautiful maps with the same curiosity that had kept her childlike ever since. "Cleo predicted this marriage." *On that unbearable day when I gave away my clothes.* "I'd go and speak to her myself, but I'm too weary to cross the room."

"I'm sure she'll be on your doorstep when she gets back to herself."

"Tell her I'll be expecting her. I want to show her the cottage."

"Eleanor," said Grace when Harley Rae had walked away, "do you mind very much that nobody brought wedding presents? I'm to blame for that too. I told them you wouldn't want to be writing thank-you notes every day till you died."

"I hope you didn't phrase it in exactly those words."

"Actually what I said was just bring food."

Eleanor smiled at her friend. "Abel and I will always be grateful to you for arranging this party, this wonderful gathering. But fifty years from now, don't do it again."

It was midafternoon before Eleanor and Abel headed for the cottage. Abigail had gone before them to Grace's house in Mr. Taylor's truck. "I wonder if he'll linger," Eleanor said.

"It looked to me like Grace was pretty taken with him."

"She was giddy all afternoon, but it might just have been wedding excitement."

"It was a fine wedding. Especially the last part."

"At the dinner?" said Eleanor.

"At the altar," he said, reaching for her hand. "We're married. Did you know that?"

"I'm beginning to know it. I wanted to remember everything, and I don't remember anything from the time I looked back at that crowd until Reverend Philbin made his announcement." She leveled a gaze on Abel. "You knew, didn't you, about the dinner."

"I did," he confessed. "The barber mentioned it. I didn't say anything because I thought it might unnerve you."

"So you waited for it to unnerve me inside the church."

"Did I make the wrong choice?"

"No." Love flooded Eleanor. "You know me better than I know myself."

"Nope, I don't. And I hope I never do. I want you to go on being whoever you are for the rest of our lives."

She put her fingers to his cheek and felt the rough stubble of his beard already growing back.

"I was moved, Abel, that so many of my old students chose to be there today. And the librarian from Payne. She said she understood now why I stopped coming on Fridays to check out books."

"You'll have to start that up again. And everything else you've let go, tending to Abby."

"When Abby goes home, she'll leave a hole in our lives."

"I think we can fill it."

He turned onto Florida Street. "There's our cottage."
His tone changed. "And we've got a visitor."

A woman huddled in a sweater was walking in the yard.

"I don't recognize her," Eleanor said.

"It's Kit," said Abel. "And I don't see Don."

"Kit! That's Kit? I thought she'd be taller. Maybe Don is
in the house."

"The house is locked."

"Oh, if only she'd come just a few hours earlier!"

Abel pulled into the drive. In a moment of flashback,
Eleanor saw herself in her nightgown, leaning out of the
truck to inspect her roof. Now Abel was her husband. And
here was his daughter. "I hope nothing has happened."

"I expect something has."

Kit hurried to the car. "Dad!" she cried. "Where have
you been?"

"Getting married," he said. "Where have you been?"

"Married!" She sent a glance like a cold hand sliding
over Eleanor. "You really know how to shock a person."

"Eleanor, this is my daughter, Mary Katherine. Mary
Katherine, my wife. If you'd come a little sooner you could
have been here for the wedding."

"You should have seen Abigail," Eleanor said. "She
wore a dress she made herself. She was our flower girl."

"You should have let me know, Dad."

"I tried to, but at the grocery-store number they said
you'd gone and they didn't know where."

"You could have called the house in Marshall. I've been
there a week."

"You said you were coming here. You and Don."

"Well, you know Don." Kit's pretty mouth twisted. "Dependable Don."

Eleanor said, "I'll go in and call Abigail. She's been longing to see you."

Ignoring Eleanor's offer, Kit began telling Abel, "We got as far as Texarkana, Dad, and Don said he wanted to look around. He'd heard there were jobs there. 'You had a job in Little Rock,' I said. 'Why didn't you just stay there?' And he said he was tired of Little Rock." Kit began crying. "So I dumped him out and went on home."

Abel put an arm around her. "It's good you had a home to go to."

She wiped her eyes with the heels of her hands. "The landlord told me you paid up through January."

"Let's go inside. You're shivering, Kit."

In a few minutes Abigail burst into the house and ran to her mother. "You missed the wedding! I prayed you would get here. I was in it!" She whirled away. "This is my dress. I made it myself! Well, I almost did. Miss Grace helped a little. Where's Dad?" She looked around. "He can't smoke, you know, in the honeymoon cottage."

"Your father is in Texarkana, Abigail."

"Are we going there?"

Kit said tiredly, "We're going home. He may come along later."

"Did you see Miss El's dress? It was her mother's."

"I saw it," said Kit. "Now, listen, honey. We have to get out of here before very long. Go get your things and we'll get on the road."

Abel looked out at the worn car parked at the curb. "It's late, Kit. Spend the night and get a fresh start in the morning."

"I want to get Abigail in school tomorrow."

"It won't hurt if I'm late. I'd like to go to school here and tell everybody good-bye. Miss El and Grampa are on their honeymoon. This is the honeymoon cottage. But you can stay with me in my room in Miss El's big house. Let's do stay, Mama!"

Eleanor, at Abel's side, said, "Please do, Kit. Stay as long as you like. There's plenty of room."

"It's not a question of room. We have to get going. We'll have a Coke first and then we'll be out of here."

"I'm afraid we don't have Coke," Eleanor said, "but we'll find something else. Abel, I think there's lemonade. Abigail and I will go gather up her things if you're certain you can't stay, Kit."

Kit turned to Abel. "Good, Dad. We'll have a few minutes to ourselves."

Where, wondered Eleanor, had Abigail learned what few manners she had? Hurrying, she caught up with Abigail skipping through the thicket.

"Do you think my mother is pretty?"

"She's very pretty." *How would this child manage? What would become of her?* "Did you tell Miss Grace your mother was here?"

Abigail ran into the house. "I think I did. I left so fast."

"You must call her before you leave. Tell her good-bye and thank her for the nice things she did for you."

"You did nice things." Abigail turned around in the door of her room, her exuberance stilled. "I didn't like you much at first. But now I love you."

Eleanor bit her lips. "What made you change your mind?"

"That day when you told me what 'gracious' means. And that I didn't have to worry about going to the poorhouse."

"I think I started loving you when we had our disagreement about entering the kitchen." Eleanor put her arms around the child and drew her close. "I'm proud of you, Abigail, and so is your grandfather. Thank you for being the perfect flower girl in your beautiful dress. I hope you will write to me."

"I will, Miss El."

"And I hope you will come back in the summer and stay with us."

"I'm getting tears on your mother's dress."

"So am I," said Eleanor. "Let's pack your things."

25

"I'd call that a whirlwind visit," Eleanor said as she and Abel stood waving at Abigail, throwing kisses out the car window.

"I'd call it a tornado," Abel said. "It was just about as depressing as one." He steered her back to the cottage and eased into Mr. Bannister's leather chair. "Now you've met Kit." He sighed. "Reckless. Impulsive. Always on the run, trying to keep her mistakes from catching up with her."

Eleanor, leaning wearily against the couch cushions, heard the sorrow in his voice. "I wish we could have persuaded her to leave Abigail with us until school is out, or at least until she gets settled."

"Kit will never be settled. Every so often we'll have to go and get her out of a jam."

"Maybe this latest experience will help her grow up."

Abel closed his eyes. "Don't I wish."

Eleanor admired tenderly the way his lanky body filled the chair her father had loved. "Did you have a chance to speak with her about anything important?"

He shook his head. "She must have known I had things to say she didn't want to hear. She only let me squeeze in hello and good-bye."

"I'm sorry, Abel."

"I'm sorry too, but she's a grown woman, and I guess we have to leave it with her. Miss El," he said, "come sit in my lap."

"In your lap! In broad daylight? What if someone comes in?"

"We're on our honeymoon, Eleanor. No one's coming in."

She went to him reluctantly. "We may break this chair down, Abel, and then you'll have to sit in that straight rocker for the rest of your life." But leaning against him she let go of the day's anxieties, thrilling to his body against hers, the smell of his skin, the safety of his arms resting loosely about her. She murmured contentedly, "I feel so at home with you."

"We are at home. We're where we belong." He kissed the curve of her ear, nibbling at it, making her shiver. "Abby is where she belongs too."

"I can't think it's good, Abel, with Kit so troubled and no father there. No job even."

"She'll find a job now that she knows she has to. Abby may be the only person Kit's ever truly loved. She needs her. And Abby needs Kit." He paused, stroking Eleanor's hair back from her forehead. "Even if we'd had time for a talk today, I wouldn't have told her I'm not her father. I'm never going to tell her, Eleanor."

"But you had made up your mind! You said everything needed to be out in the open."

"What good would it do out in the open? You saw her," he said. "Who would it help if I told her now?"

"You, that's who! You've been carrying that burden far too long."

"So I should shift it to her? Just to set the record straight?"

"Telling the truth is never wrong."

"Sometimes it's unnecessary. The truth can't give Kit another father this late in the day. She has no mother. No husband. Abby is all the family she has."

Eleanor said crisply, "Well, she certainly didn't take to her new stepmother."

Abel chuckled. "You didn't take to me either, the first time you saw me."

"Yes, I did." Eleanor twitched uncomfortably. "I just didn't let on."

Abel kissed her ear again. "Maybe underneath Kit's rudeness she's not letting on either. Maybe she's afraid she'll be out of the picture now that you're in it."

Eleanor frowned. "I suppose that's possible."

"I expect she was a little jealous too, that Abby was happy with us."

"She knows nothing about Abby's pain, the tears she shed when she didn't hear from her mother. That was mean and selfish, Abel, to ignore the child."

"Granted, she should have stayed in touch with Abby, and with us too, for that matter. And I didn't hear any thanks for looking after her daughter. I'm sure it never occurred to her that she interrupted our lives or that having a child to care for all this time might have been too much for us. She's selfish, yes, but I wouldn't say she's intentionally mean. She's poorly trained. She needed guidance, and she didn't get it from her mother. Or from me."

Eleanor kissed his cheek. "You gave her a priceless gift. You needn't feel guilty about anything."

They sat quietly for a time, listening to the wind blowing against the shutters. Then Abel said, "You may be right. She may grow up yet. She may, as they say, 'come around.'"

Eleanor turned slowly to face her husband. "If I could have anything in the world, I would choose to be as kind as you are, Abel Brown. Is there any hope, do you think, that I may 'come around'?"

He kissed her gently. "If I could have anything in the world I'd choose you every time, just like you are."

In a while they moved to the kitchen. Halting in the middle of the floor, Eleanor exclaimed, "There's nothing here to eat except breakfast cereal! I didn't think once about food *after* the wedding!"

"It's not a fatal error," Abel soothed. "We'll go through the thicket to our other house. We'll pretend it's a restaurant. Except we won't have champagne."

"We'll have wine, if I can remember where I put the bottle I didn't bring out the first time we ate together. A good thing too. It gave me a headache."

"Then we'll skip the wine. No headaches tonight."

The telephone rang as they were starting out the door.

"Grace," sighed Eleanor.

"Surely not."

She held out the phone so he could hear for himself.

"Excuse me!" Grace said. "I hope I haven't interrupted anything personal, but I had to call. I have supper plates ready for you, food from the reception and two slices of wedding cake I set aside. Not a bite was left. It was wonderful cake! That delicious pineapple filling, and so much good icing! I do love icing, but you know that, don't you? Oh, and I want to tell you it did my heart good to see how happy our little girl was when her mother came—late, but anyway she got herself here."

"Grace. Thank you." Eleanor looked at Abel with raised eyebrows. "One of us will be over to get the plates."

"No, no! There's no need for that. Bill Taylor is just leaving. He'll drop them off at your door." She suppressed a giggle. "Unless you and Abel are otherwise engaged."

"We are through being engaged, Grace. We are married now."

"You know what I mean!"

"When is Mr. Taylor coming?"

"In the next five minutes. As a matter of fact," she added excitedly, "I'll be with him. We're going to the movies."

Dark came and they were still at the table, still in their wedding clothes, discussing things: Mr. Taylor and Grace. And Abel's idea that he and Mr. Taylor might start up a little repair business, carpentering and such.

Eleanor objected to that. "I don't want you climbing around, falling off ladders."

"I didn't notice you worrying about that when I was working on the cottage."

"Things are different now."

"I believe they are."

"On the other hand, I don't want you underfoot all day."

He hid his smile with a yawn. "No need to decide everything tonight. Let's leave the kitchen as it is and go to bed."

Eleanor rose quickly. "You go ahead. I want to rinse off the dishes and straighten up a bit."

Abel stretched. "Kiss me good-night?"

"Just a peck," she said. "I don't want to spoil you."

He bent to receive her airy kiss and ambled toward his bedroom. "Sleep well, Eleanor."

"I'm sure I shall. I'm half asleep now."

But she was wide awake when she finished in the kitchen. At the open door of Abel's room, she paused for a moment. The light was on by his bed, but his eyes were closed. She hesitated another minute and then moved on.

In her own room, she undressed slowly with the door closed. *Why didn't it occur to me to buy a new nightgown? In case there's a fire and I have to run out?*

In the bathroom she dawdled, examining her face, combing her hair. Noting her heart rate. Up quite a bit.

Well, of course it was up! With the wedding and all. Meeting Kit. Losing Abigail. Maybe she ought to take an aspirin.

Deciding against medication, she returned to her room after another brief glance at Abel, at the length of him beneath the quilt, one hand atop it, relaxed fingers laid across his stomach.

Climbing into her own bed, she pulled up the covers and turned out the light, aware of her thudding heart as she stared into the darkness.

He is not going to call me, not going to insist on anything.

She turned over to face the window. Then back toward the door, where faint light shone from Abel's room beyond the bathroom.

The first night of marriage is the same as any other night. My husband might as well be sleeping in the trailer for all the difference a wedding made!

She sat up, trembling. *Perspiring a little. In the middle of winter!*

Tossing back her quilt, she got out of bed and padded into Abel's room. She put out the light and crawled in beside him.

Abel stirred and took her hand.

She said, "It's the right thing, isn't it?"

He murmured in her ear, "It's exactly the right thing."

They lay quietly, white space between them, and years of living separately.

"What do you see, Abel, when you close your eyes?"

"Black snakes usually. Dancing the hula."

She smiled in the dark. "I see faces."

"Anybody you know?"

"They change constantly, man to woman, child to adult."

"Probably," he said, "it's our blood-pressure medicine."

His thumb stroked her palm.

"Were you asleep, Abel?

"I wasn't," he said, talking softly in the silence of the cottage, of the nuptial bed. "I was thinking of Don."

"Why weren't you thinking of me?"

"I was, actually. I was thinking of what a worry Don is to Kit—and the worry I've been to you, always making you wonder when you woke up if I'd be gone."

"I've made peace with that, Abel. I won't like it, but I can bear it."

"You can forget it, Eleanor. All these months it's been coming clear to me like a piece of film in a pan of developer."

"What has, Abel?"

"The reason I've roamed all my life."

Every nerve end tingled. "What is the reason?"

"I was looking for you."

She moved against him. "And I was here. Waiting."